BAREBACK RANGE
A Novel Set On The Prairies

by Frank Sol

Copyright 2004 Cosmic Legends Publishing

Drafts2Digitial Edition, License Notes

This is a work of fiction. Names, characters, places, and incidents are products of the author's imagination or are used fictitiously and are not to be construed as real. Any resemblance to actual events, locales, organizations, or persons, living or dead, is entirely coincidental.

Content warning: For adult readers over the age of 18 only. This book contains explicit sexual situations between two men.

The characters portrayed are of legal age for sexual consent within Canada.

Cover Model—Austin

Chapter One

"Morning, Constable." Clint had watched the marked cruiser roll up the long drive towards his barn. He had finished tying two saddlebags onto his horse while waiting. *No time to stand around idle while waiting for him to get here.* The farm and the surrounding prairie were fairly flat and morning sunlight glinting off the car's windshield had caught his attention long before the sound of its engine reached him.

"Morning, Clint." Constable Steven Daniels climbed out of his car and stretched out his arms and his back. He was a big man, over six feet tall, and the cruiser just seemed too small for him. He gave Clint a polite nod. "You're looking busy." Sunglasses hid his eyes.

"Got some fences to mend. Had to get out for an early start." Clint adjusted his white *Stetson* to better shade his dark eyes. The top three buttons on the constable's uniform shirt were undone, to better catch the warm breeze. *It is shaping up to be a mighty fine spring day.* "Don't often see you out this way." He gave his mare an absentminded pat on her grey-coloured flanks.

"I was just passing by. Got some complaints back in town yesterday so I had to take a run out here and at least put in an appearance." He hooked his thumb back towards the east, and then pulled off his sunglasses. "Figured I might as well check up on you seeing as I was just up the road a spell."

"Thanks for the concern." Clint nodded, not taking his eyes off the uniformed police officer. *Damn, he fills out that uniform nicely. Wouldn't mind getting myself frisked by him sometime.* "Complaints, ya say?" he prompted.

"Some chickens have gone missing."

"Chickens?" The old cowboy threw his head back and laughed. "Constance dragged you way the hell out here for some missing chickens? Or was it Sally?" He shook his head. "You ain't got time for shooting coyotes."

"Coyotes don't steal the Saturday washing off the line."

After a moment, Clint nodded his agreement with that. "True." He stuck his hands into the back pockets of his *Levis* and then leaned against the rail fence.

"This is one of them two-legged varmints. I thought you should be on the lookout." The constable gestured to the pasture and the wheat fields beyond. The Rocky Mountains rose on the horizon. "You're quite a ways out of town, Clint. You've got no neighbours close by...course I know you like your privacy."

"Yep."

"Still, you should take some precautions."

"I'll keep my old Winchester handy. No thief—two-legged or otherwise—is gonna take anything from me."

The constable's dark eyes travelled up and down the length of Clint's frame. "Yep, we've *all* heard about that *big* gun of yours."

"Better than that six shooter I hear you keep." Clint tossed that back with a grin.

Daniels ruefully shook his head. "Just don't go shooting anyone's prize bull."

"That was just a heifer and it was straying onto my land. Took me by surprise when she burst out of the scrub." Clint spat onto the dusty ground. "Shoot, Steven, that was damn near twenty years ago."

Daniels nodded. "Yep, it was." He nodded and adjusted his hat. "I'd just made deputy and you were the first complaint I had to deal with."

"Didn't want you to get bored with your job."

"Boredom can be good." Steven adjusted his hat. "If I wanted to be busy, I'd have applied for a transfer to Calgary or Edmonton. Plenty of police work in the big cities."

"True. Plenty of work on a farm too." Clint shook his head. *Gotta paint that barn this summer.*

"I like living in a small town."

"Do ya?"

"I know everyone." Daniels shrugged. "I know the troublemakers and where to find them when I need to have a little chat with any of them. What's the worst crime I have to deal with?"

"Sure not cattle rustling."

Daniels chuckled. "Usually just got a few rowdy cowboys after the Saloon closes Saturday night."

Clint rechecked the buckle on the saddlebag. "Be a pleasure to stand here and shoot the breeze all day, but I got work to be about." *It* would *be a pleasure to shoot* something *with him!* "I'll keep my eyes open for your varmint, Constable. Safe ride back."

"Take care, Clint." The constable nodded to him one more, and then headed back towards his cruiser.

While his back was turned, Clint gave his crotch a quick rub, to try and adjust his stiff hard-on behind the fly of his jeans. *Damn, Steven always does that to me.*

With a quick honk from the cruiser's horn, the constable drove off.

Clint sighed and lit up a cigarette.

Chapter Two

Clint turned off the radio and lit up a cigarette. "Ain't playing anything good," he muttered as he turned off the ceiling light and plunged the room into semi-darkness. He walked from the kitchen table to check the fire. Along with warming the great room, the fireplace was also providing most of the ambient light. The night was still cool for late March; a chilly wind had been gusting down from the north since before the sun had set. "It should storm soon. Come down in buckets I reckon." He was used to talking to himself. *Too many years of living alone out here,* he thought with wry smile. "Need some rain for the garden. I'm getting too old to carry water from the well for all them plants." He stared through the big window out into the darkness.

The stars were out, plainly visible in the night sky. The barn was a just a dark shape against the horizon.

Out in the pasture beside the barn, one of the cows mooed.

"Shit." Clint tossed his spent cigarette into the fireplace, then took a long twig from a jar on the mantle and lit the end of it. He used the impromptu match to light a lantern hanging near the door, and then headed out into the yard, rifle in hand.

The night chill was present, but not quite cold enough to send him back inside for his jacket. *Not for just a quick walk to the barn and back.* His breath puffed out in front of him and he paused a moment to watch it in the moonlight. The grass rustled under his boots as he started walking again. The lantern was something he hardly needed outside—Clint had walked this land since he was a baby. He knew every fold and gopher hole.

The barn was quiet.

Too quiet. Clint pulled the door open—it creaked and he made a mental note to oil it in the morning—and stepped inside. The air was heavy with the smell of hay and dust and manure and just the faintest hint of cigarette smoke. He hung the lantern on a nail near the door and then pulled the door closed behind him.

Out in the field, one of the cows mooed again.

Two horses lifted their heads to look at him in sleepy surprise. Normally he left them alone after stabling them for the night. The grey mare went back to eating out of a bucket of oats. The roan stallion just snorted and pawed at the floor of his stall.

Clint took the lantern down from the nail and he surveyed the inside of the barn. Everyone looked to be where he had left it earlier. With measured steps, he walked past the two occupied stalls towards the empty ones at the back. His boots clicked softly on the stone floor. He stopped and peered into one stall, seeing nothing but a surprised field mouse, then he hung the lantern on a hook and turned around to the other stall.

He pulled the gate open with one hand and pointed the rifle in. "What you doing in my barn?" he demanded.

A boy was huddled in one corner, half-buried in the straw, staring back at him from under the brim of a tan-coloured cowboy hat. He looked frightened and a bit desperate.

Clint kept the rifle pointed towards him.

"I don't want no trouble," the youth said in a soft voice.

"Neither do I, boy. That's why I got this after all." He hefted the rifle as he spoke. "So what you after?"

"Nothing," he shook his head. "I was just looking for a place to spend the night."

"In my barn?"

"It's warm and dry."

Clint eyed him. "You're not from around here."

"No."

Stepping out of the lantern's light, Clint could see now that what he thought was just a young boy was actually a young handsome man, probably in his mid-twenties. *Though it's hard to tell under all that grime on his face.* "What's your name?"

"Jesse."

Clint's eyes narrowed. "Got a last name?"

"Helmer. Jesse Helmer."

"I'm Clint Baxter." He flipped the rifle up to rest on his shoulder. "You can't sleep out here. You'll frighten the horses. Come up to the house. There's some spare rooms there where you can bunk yourself down."

Jesse didn't move.

"It's either that or out in the pasture with the cows. You ain't sleeping in my barn."

"I'll take the bunk."

"Good choice. Come on then. I don't plan to be out here all night."

"Thank you." Jesse grabbed a small bundle from the straw beside him and followed Clint.

"A word of advice. If you're gonna try to hide in a barn, give up smoking. That match glows brighter than any firefly. Too early in the season for fireflies."

Jesse kicked at a stone with his boot as they walked across the grass. "I was wondering how you'd found me."

"I know a lot of tricks, boy." Clint stepped through the doorway and hung his rifle on a pair of hooks on the wall. "You look cold."

"I'm okay." Jesse rubbed his arms through the long sleeves of his blue shirt as he spoke though.

"You can set your stuff over there for now."

Jesse dropped his bundle on the floor near the wall. It didn't look like the tied-up shirt contained very much at all.

A single change of clothes at best. This boy sure travels light. Clint hooked a thumb towards a doorway across the room. "Washroom through there if you want to clean up. Down the hallway on the left."

"Thank you." Jesse hurried through the door.

Clint snorted. He filled a small kettle and then put it onto the wood stove.

When Jesse returned to the kitchen, Clint set a mug of hot coffee in front of him. "This'll take the night's chill off ya." Clint gave the young man a closer inspection. *He cleans up real nice,* he thought.

Jesse looked to be in his late twenties. He had scrubbed the dirt from his face and the few days' growth of dark stubble on his cheeks gave him some character. A puffy bruise coloured his left cheek. His green t-shirt was dirty, as were his torn jeans, but his hands were now mostly clean. He had discarded his grimy blue shirt on top of his small bundle, along with his hat.

Some dirt you just can't rinse away, Clint thought. *Nature of farm life. It just stays under your fingernails.* He shambled away from the table, his worn black boots clicking on the old wooden floorboards. "Drink up. The nights are still too damned cold for this time of the year."

Jesse took the mug and took a drink before replying. "That's why I snuck into your barn. I was freezing last night trying to sleep under the stars."

"Got no sleeping roll?"

"Nope."

Clint brought a few slices of bread and some yellowish cheddar to the table and set them down in front of his impromptu guest. "Where you from?"

"A little town near Medicine Hat. Redcliff."

"I've heard of it." Clint sipped his own mug of coffee and watched Jesse stuff an entire slice of bread into his mouth at once. "You're a long way from home then."

"I have my reasons," Jesse mumbled around the half-chewed bread.

Clint granted him a few moments of peace to gorge himself. *Not been eating too well it looks like,* he noted. *Wonder if he's got a hairy chest?* He gave his head a shake. *Stop thinking shit like that,* he told himself. "Why you running?"

Jesse froze in mid-bite. "Who says I'm running?"

"You got the look." He paused a moment. "You're also, what two hundred clicks from home?"

Jesse swallowed his mouthful.

Clint sipped at his coffee. "You ain't a local boy. You ain't visiting anyone around here cause you'd be there and not camping out in my barn, molesting my milkers."

"I didn't touch your animals."

Clint's mouth twisted into a grin. "I know...the horses were settled down for the night and they would've raised a ruckus if you'd bothered either of them."

"I'll be gone in the morning."

Clint allowed the silence to drag out for a few moments. "Not so fast, boy," he said. "You're staying under my roof tonight. You're eating my food. You owe me something in exchange."

Jesse shook his head sadly. "I got no cash on me. I can't pay you for the bed."

"You can work it off. I got chores. Lord, do I got chores around this place."

Jesse licked the last crumbs from his fingers. "Chores huh?"

"Yep." Clint nodded. He watched Jesse as the young man looked around, giving the place a casual appraisal. It was a fairly typical farmhouse with a big kitchen that blended directly into the living room. The furnishings were plain and most were home-crafted. Everything was clean. "How old are you?"

He hesitated for a long moment, staring down at the torn knee of his jeans. "Twenty-five."

Shit, I'm old enough to be his father, Clint thought with annoyance. He himself had just turned thirty-nine. *Well, maybe his brother*, he amended a moment later. *His much older brother.*

Jesse yawned.

"I'll show you where you're bunking down."

"Thanks, Clint." Jesse scooped up his small bundle and followed Clint down the short hallway.

Chapter Three

Clint woke up, half-expecting the farmhouse to be empty. For a few moments, he just lay there listening to the sounds of the farm. Chickens tended to be noisy and cows were little better. He was sporting some serious morning wood and gave his hard dick a few strokes, more from habit than from any real need. Jesse's face kept drifting into his thoughts. *That boy sure is a cute one,* he thought. *I wonder if he sleeps naked?* The bed springs groaned as he shifted position, but Jesse was bunked on the far side of the house, well out of earshot.

Finally Clint gave up and tossed the blankets aside and stood up, buck-naked. He stared into the mirror hanging on the wall. He had a nice, well-muscled frame, tanned from years spent in the sun. For a guy pushing forty, he looked good.

The old farmhouse seemed awfully quiet.

Clint sighed and headed into the bathroom. "Guess he took off."

He pulled his jeans on after leaving the bathroom though and walked down the short hallway into the kitchen. *Just in case.*

Jesse was nowhere to be seen.

Clint snorted. "I thought as much." He gave the great room a quick glance over, but nothing seemed to be missing. *Not like I got much worth stealing,* he thought. He turned to the wood stove. It was already lit and the kettle sitting on top of it was hot.

Jesse pulled open the kitchen door and stepped inside, holding a small basket. "How you like your eggs?" he asked with a cheerful smile. "I found five, at least."

Clint nodded. "Them hens is good at hiding them."

"You need a proper chicken coop."

Clint shook his head. "I like to let them have free run. I don't like caging things. Never have." He shrugged, dismissing his quirks. "Is that coffee I smell?"

"Yep." Jesse nodded. "I figured you'd want some. Got fresh milk in the jug there."

"You milked Bertie?"

"Yeah. The bucket was easy to find and she was waiting for me when I went out to look for those damned chickens."

Clint nodded. "You seem to know your way around a farm."

"This ain't my first time out in the country."

"Glad to see you making yourself useful."

"You said I owed you." Jesse finished cracking the eggs into a bowl and gave them a vigorous stir.

"You sleep good?" Clint watched the way his butt moved under his snug *Wranglers* as he stirred milk and pepper into the eggs. *Damn nice sight to see.*

"Yes, better than I have for weeks. That bed was real warm. Slept like a log."

"Good. I don't know the last time it was used." Tearing his eyes off Jesse, Clint walked over to the stove and poured himself a mug of the coffee and then downed half of it in a long swallow. "I don't have the hired help my grandpa used to have to run this place. He worked a lot of acres, ran more than a thousand head most years."

"I wondered where everyone was." Jesse nodded towards the east wing where he had slept. "There're so many rooms in this place."

"Grandma believed that the hired help was as worthy as family. She made sure each man got a good meal and a warm place to sleep." Clint yawned. "The house is too big for me...I don't use half the rooms." *This damned house is awful lonely sometimes.* "That whole wing for example." His bedroom was built off the kitchen, in the south end of the rambling farmhouse. "The bunk rooms were added by my grandpa decades ago, before I was born."

Jesse set a frying pan onto the stove. "So, how you like your eggs?"

"Surprise me."

Jesse chuckled "I thought I'd already done that."

Clint shook his head. "Thought I'd wake up and find you gone." He walked over to one of the cupboards and pulled out some old chipped plates.

"You sound disappointed that I'm still here."

"Nope," Clint protested. "You stay, you stay. If you'd run off..." he shrugged. "Can't make you stay here."

"I could use a few days' rest before moving on," Jesse admitted. "Been a long journey so far."

Jesse lifted the frying pan off the stove.

Jesse dumped the dishes into the sink.

Clint sipped at his coffee and then took a quick drag on his cigarette. He licked his lips as Jesse bent over the sink to wash up the plates.

His snug green t-shirt stretched taunt against his back and his jeans moulded themselves to his ass.

"You seem pretty handy."

"My mom taught me to be a good guest."

"You're a credit to her then."

Jesse turned from the sink and wiped his hands on a towel. "You said you got some chores for me?"

"Yep." Clint grabbed a blue checked shirt from where it hung on the back of a chair. The table could seat a dozen easy; he couldn't recall the last time he'd had anyone else eat a meal with him. He pulled the shirt on and buttoned it up as he paced across the floor. "How are you at carrying water buckets?"

* * *

"So you got all this land and you live out here alone?"

"Yep. Most of the land I got is range for the cows and horses. Not much call for men to work them all of the time...and when I need some hired help, I can usually rustle it up from town." Clint had let the two horses out of the barn and into the pasture and now he closed the gate behind them. "I live alone cause that's how I like it." He hooked his finger towards the corner. "Shovel and wheelbarrow are over there."

"Okay." Jesse nodded. He hung his hat on a nail inside the door.

The open doors allowed plenty of sunlight to light the barn's interior. The wind was blowing from the right direction to blow through the barn as well, airing out the interior. More shafts of light filtered through cracks in the walls and showed dust motes floating in the air.

"The folks in town said to stay away from you." Jesse paused a moment, before grabbing the shovel. "They were talking about you at the coffee shop. They told me you were supposed to be trouble."

Clint chuckled. "The constable was out here a few days ago. He told me the same thing about you. Course, back then we thought you was just a coyote who stole laundry as well as chickens."

Looking sheepish, Jesse bowed his head and stared at down at his blue jeans. "Sometimes," he said in a quiet tone, "men have gotta do things they'd rather not."

Clint nodded. "Yep. Don't make them right though."

"I know." Jesse tried to brush dirt from his thigh, but it was too ingrained. "I heard in town that you sleep with a shotgun in your bed."

"They told ya about old Winnie?" Clint laughed. "Winnie hangs on the wall." He gestured towards the farmhouse where the rifle waited. "Everyone knows ya keep a *Colt Forty-Five* under your pillow."

Chapter Four

"I borrowed one of your razors," Jesse said over breakfast the next morning. He ran his hand along his freshly-shaven cheek. "Hope you don't mind."

Clint grunted as he drank his morning coffee.

"I guess I should head into town one of these days and pick some things up." Jesse brushed at the legs of his jeans, but they were fairly dirty and his half-hearted brushing had no obvious effects. His grey t-shirt was travel-stained as well.

"Be making a trip to Nanton in a couple of days." Clint set his mug onto the table. "I don't go into town much. Can't be bothered wasting the gas to get there."

Jesse nodded. "Understandable. It's a lot nicer out here."

"Yep." Clint was surprised to hear the younger man say that. He commented that he didn't hold with a lot of the new fangled toys people had to have.

"Yeah, I didn't see any sign of a computer or a satellite dish."

"Got no use for t.v. Got no time to waste on learning a computer. Always plenty of chores to keep a man busy."

"Early to bed, early to rise?"

"Yep. My grandma swore by that saying."

Jesse lit up a cigarette. He looked into his almost empty pack and sighed.

"You've done a fine job of mucking out the stables yesterday. I don't think I've seen them look that clean in years."

Jesse shrugged. "I just tried to do my best."

"Well keep it up. Anyway, we got a fence to work on fixing up today."

* * *

Jesse was hammering nails into the pole to hold the fence slats in place.

Clint rode up on the back of his roan stallion. He had been watching from a distance for a while now, enjoying the sight of the younger man working hard.

Jesse was shirtless in the heat of the day—the ever-unpredictable Alberta weather had brought them an early heat wave—and his body was already bronzed from past days of working in the sun. He had a lean body, well muscled without being overly so, the body of a hard worker.

Clint's eyes narrowed as he took in the signs of bruising on the man's ribs. The thick dark hair helped to mask most of the fading bruises, but his close inspection didn't miss seeing them.

Jesse paused a moment to stretch, then went right back to work.

Mm, I do love a man with a hairy chest. Jesse had a thick coat of brown fur across his pecks and trailing down to his waist. "Yep, a fine stud."

"Sorry?" Jesse turned around.

"The bull," Clint hastily said as he pulled his eyes away from Jesse's hairy chest and back up to his face. He gestured to the nearby pasture. "He's a good stud."

"Oh. I'm almost done here."

"You're working hard." Clint had started out working alongside Jesse to get the job underway and make sure that the other man understood how the repairs were to be done; but Clint had left him alone while taking his horse for a quick ride along the fence to check for other places in need of repair. "Good news, the rest of the fence is fine. We just have this section to fix."

"That is good news."

This time Clint saw him wince, as he did stand erect and stretch out his back again. *What happened to him?* he wondered. *Someone tried to beat the shit out of him.*

* * *

The constable's cruiser pulled up the drive, raising a plume of dust.

Steven Daniels got out of the car and nodded casually to the young man pushing a straw-filled wheelbarrow out of the barn. "Morning." He adjusted his hat.

"Hello, Constable." The man nodded a quick greeting, and then picked up his pace and hurriedly vanished behind the barn.

Daniels watched him disappear, then chuckled softly. His eyes were hidden behind his sunglasses, but he didn't miss anything.

Clint came out of the farmhouse. "Morning, Constable," he called from the porch. "You out here on business again?"

"Morning, Clint." Steven Daniels walked towards the house. "Got yourself a new hired hand?" It wasn't really a question.

"Yep." Clint nodded. He leaned back against the side of the house and rested his hands on his belt buckle. "You still out chasing that two-legged coyote?"

"Not this time."

"Good to hear. Not been any sign of any thievery out my way."

"Nothing new from your neighbours either," Steven admitted. "I was just...curious as to how you were making out."

"Just fine."

"No shooting off of that big gun of yours?"

"None at all. No targets for it."

"Good, good." Steven stepped over a rut in the driveway. "There was an interesting rumour going around the *Tim Horton's* last night," he commented as he came around the front bumper of Clint's old Chevy

"Oh?"

"Folks down there were talking about seeing a new face up here. Folks wondered if you'd gotten yourself a new hired hand."

"Christ. He's only been here three days."

"And people are already talking." Daniels chuckled at Clint's annoyed expression. "Good to see you doing your part to keep folks entertained."

Clint swore.

Daniels just shrugged in response. "So what's his story?"

"Son of an old schoolmate," Clint told him. "He was just passing through on his way up north. Stopped to sleep in my barn and I caught him there. Didn't know who I was at the time, just looking for a warm place to sleep. I offered him a job helping with some of the chores 'round here. It's still a big farm."

"You found this guy in your barn and then just offered him a job?"

Clint grimaced and shrugged. "Sometimes a guy needs a helping hand to get back on his feet," he said defensively. "Nothing wrong with that."

"Oh, I agree. Maybe I should speak with him myself. I'd like to hear his story about where he came from. He's not a local boy."

"Nope, came from down south."

"So can I talk to him?"

"No need to interrupt him. I got him working hard."

"Riding his ass, are you?"

Clint snorted.

"You know how gossip travels around a small town like Nanton."

"Don't I," Clint agreed, not bothering to mask the irritation he felt. "A man's got no privacy to take a shit without folks talking."

Daniels hardly blinked at that comment.

"So some busybody drove past and saw Jesse working on my farm and now the whole town is talking about him?"

"Something like that."

"Probably Sally. She's got a big mouth."

"I have heard that..."

Clint eyed the other man from under the brim of his *Stetson*. "Pity she never stops flapping her gums long enough to put her mouth to something useful."

Daniels smiled wryly.

"So now you can go and share some of your own gossip tonight with your evening coffee at *Timmy's*. Set the record straight."

"This Jesse, he's just a hired hand? Son of an old friend you say?"

"Yep. I'll vouch for him. If anything's gone missing in the last week, I'll swear on a stack of Bibles that it wasn't took by him. He's not been off the ranch all week. Had no time to get up to anything. I've been working him hard." Clint shifted position. "Not that it's any business of folks."

"Quite." The constable brushed imaginary lint from the front of his navy blue uniform. "I should be getting along then. I've got a route to patrol after all."

"Won't keep ya then." Clint nodded to him. "Leave us real men to our work."

Daniels shook his head, and then sauntered back to his car.

Does he put that extra sway in his walk just to torment me? Clint wondered. *It's a wonder he hasn't split the ass out of those pants, he wears 'em so snug.*

Daniels closed the door and started the engine. It started with a loud rumble and then the car drove back down the driveway.

Jesse pushed the wheelbarrow back into sight. "Is he gone?"

"Yep, he just left." Clint lit up a cigarette. "When you get around to telling me your story, it had better be a damned good one. Cause I just lied to the law for you and I don't cover nobody's ass. Why I did it for you, I don't know."

Jesse looked down at the ground. He kicked at a clod of dirt with his scuffed up boot.

Clint brushed past him. "Best get back to the barn and finish your work, boy."

"I was mucking out the stable like you told me too."

"Good to see you keeping busy."

"I'm doing my best to earn my keep."

Chapter Five

"I can't recall if I ever introduced you. This is Railjumper."

"You didn't call him Railrider?"

Clint shook his head and patted the roan's flanks. "He was a feisty colt...had myself quite a time breaking him in. I managed it though. Never met a beast I couldn't master."

Jesse nodded. "Nice horse. Good piece of horseflesh."

Clint had saddled his stallion and now he was tying one onto the grey mare. "This is Misty Morning. I've had her for years now. Hard worker, like you. Good old girl. She's probably more your speed." He turned to look at the other man. "You ride, don't ya?"

"Course I do," Jesse replied indignantly.

"Okay then." Clint smiled and settled himself into the saddle of his own horse. "Nothing like having a stallion between your legs."

Jesse was climbing into the mare's saddle, and he stopped halfway into the stirrup to laugh. "I'd rather be hung like a stallion," he replied.

"Yeah, that's nice too."

Jesse shifted position slightly, and took a grip on the reins.

Misty Morning neighed.

"Hold the reins tightly, boy! You have to show 'em who's in charge." He had a firm grip on the Railjumper's reins. "Be gentle, but firm."

"Got it."

Misty Morning suddenly snorted and took off at a gallop.

"Jesse!" Clint slapped the reins on Railjumper. "Jesse!"

* * *

The damned mare sure travelled ground fast, Clint noted as he rode after his hired hand. She hadn't slowed from her gallop across the field, not matter what her rider yelled or how he tugged on the reins that he was holding in a white-knuckled grip.

"Whoa!" Jesse yelled.

Clint shook his head. *I didn't know the old girl still had it in her.* He spurred his horse to gallop faster. "Come on, Rail."

The mare was galloping along a wooden rail fence.

Clint wondered if Jesse recognized the area from where he had been working early that week. *We're getting near the old pond,* he thought. *Maybe she'll stop there for a drink.* He sure *hoped* she stopped for a drink. He could dimly hear Jesse yelling something from a distance. *At least he knows I'm following.*

The pond came into view and the mare showed no signs of stopping.

"Whoa!" Jesse screamed.

The mare suddenly stopped at the edge of the pond and caught off guard, Jesse went flying from her back. He landed in the pond with a tremendous splash.

Bare moments later, Clint rode up on his own steed. "You all right?" he demanded as Railjumper pawed at the ground.

Jesse stood up. "Fuck, that's cold!" Jesse shook his head to clear it, then reached up to brush his soaking wet hair from in front of his brown eyes. He grabbed his tan-coloured hat from where it floated next to him. "Damn it." He stuck it onto his head.

"I thought you said you could ride?" Clint was trying hard not to laugh. His heart was pounding, but Jesse didn't seem to be hurt. He did look awfully bedraggled though. "Thought you said you'd been on a horse before."

"I was." Jesse sloshed his way out of the pond. "Years ago when my folks took me to the Stampede. I was given one of those pony rides."

"At the Stampede?" Clint shook his head. "Shit."

Jesse laughed ruefully. "Guess I need a little more practice."

"At least you stayed in the saddle. I'd have thought you'd fallen off miles back."

"Nope, I got a good grip on the reins and didn't know enough to let go." Jesse tossed his hat onto the ground. Then he peeled his grey t-shirt up over his head and wrung it out. He shivered as the breeze played across his torso.

Clint licked his lips as he took in the younger man's hairy muscular chest. The hair was matted and slicked down and it made Jesse look even sexier. "As long as you're all right." Jesse's slender legs were half-visible as the soaked denim moulded itself to him. *He's looking mighty all right.* He felt a stirring his loins as he watched.

Jesse pulled his t-shirt back on, not bothering to tuck it back into his jeans, and the thin cotton clung tightly to his chest. He snatched his hat up from the ground. "Come here, you stupid animal." He stalked towards the mare.

Clint stared into the pond. The waters stilled and he saw his reflection. "Shit, when did I get so old?" he asked. *I'm lusting after a guy fifteen years younger than me!*

* * *

"You in here?"

No answer.

Clint pushed open the door. The bunk room, like the rest of the east wing, was deserted. He walked over to the bed. It was neatly made. "The boy's got manners and good sense," he observed in satisfaction. "Can't stand a messy house."

There were pegs lined along one of the walls, but only a handful of clothes were hanging on them.

Sunlight coming through the window caught on a spider web in the corner of the frame.

Clint looked at the clothes. One shirt, the faded blue one that Jesse had been wearing over his t-shirt that first night, one pair of blue jeans, a green t-shirt and a once-white one. *Add that to what the kid's got on right now....* "He sure don't own much."

The kitchen door slammed.

"Clint, you ready for some breakfast?"

"Yeah," Clint called out.

Jesse appeared in the doorway to the kitchen and Clint stepped back out into the hallway. "What's going on?"

"I was just going to wash some of my clothes. Thought I'd toss yours in as well."

"Thanks," Jesse replied. "Guess I don't have too many changes of clothes to worry about."

Clint had already gathered up the few things in the room. "What about those you got on?" he asked. "They're getting pretty dirty."

"They're all I got," Jesse replied as he looked down at himself. "They're not too bad really...they got rinsed off in the pond at least," he finished with a shy smile.

Clint nodded. "True." He hooked his thumb towards the other side of the house. "Still, you can't wear 'em forever. They're gonna start smelling. You can borrow some of my duds for the day. Give me a chance to clean those up."

"Well..."

"I insist. If you're gonna be working around here, you need something clean to wear."

Over in his bedroom, Clint pulled a shirt off the peg. "This should fit you," he said. "We look to be about the same size. Well, near-enough."

"Yeah, I guess so." With that, Jesse peeled his grey t-shirt shirt over his head. The fading bruises on his ribs were pretty much invisible now. His hands dropped down to his belt.

Clint swallowed as the belt was pulled out of its loops and tossed onto his bed.

"Thanks, Clint." Jesse unzipped his *Levi's*.

"I'll be in the kitchen," he said, looking away before he saw more than a glimpse of Jesse's white briefs. He hurried through the door, trying not to turn around. *Mmm, but I want too!* "Just call me when you're ready."

Jesse walked into the kitchen, feeling a bit self-conscious in another man's clothes. He wasn't used to sharing. The tan shirt was a little baggy on him, but the blue jeans fit fairly well.

Clint nodded and then turned back to tub of water he had boiled. "Just toss 'em in here," he told the other man. "Put another pot on the stove and brew us up some coffee."

"I can do that."

Chapter Six

Jesse was digging up the ground in what would become a small vegetable garden.

Clint stood and watched him for a while. *One thing to say about him, he sure works a hard day.* Over the last few days, Jesse had already proven himself no stranger to hard work, always being quietly efficient and always knowing what to do next without having to be told. *He's as country-oriented as I am.* Clint nodded with satisfaction.

He had taken off his shirt in the early April heat and Clint enjoyed watching the muscles on his back move as he dug the pitchfork into the ground and then broke up the clumps of dirt. His borrowed jeans rode low on his hips.

Mmm. "At least you know which is weeds," Clint said aloud. Jesse had avoided part of the garden where some of the perennial plants were starting to turn green.

Jesse left the pitchfork dug into the ground and turned around. "I used to weed my mom's garden."

"Did you do a good job of it?"

"I'd sweat my ass off while she sat on her porch and read out of her Bible."

"A Bible thumper. Can't stand those." Clint spat into the dust. *It's a nice ass though.* "My grandma taught me to know my plants. Grandpa ran the cattle, but she kept the food for us."

"Thanks for washing my things," Jesse said after a moment.

"Your blue jeans are actually blue. Imagine that." Clint chuckled, then sobered. "I don't need you stinking up my house like an old barn," he said gruffly.

* * *

Clint rolled over. He stared up the exposed beams of the ceiling. Moonlight played off of them.

He couldn't stop thinking about Jesse. "Hired hand," he told himself. "Nothing more." Jesse was just so much like an old schoolmate of his, Jason...how many years had it been? More than twenty? *And I'm still thinking about him.* And still missing him...

It was nearing the end of June, that long ago summer, and Clint was at the farm by himself. His folks had gone out of town for the weekend, on business. They'd left their son to his own devices. *'Just don't forget to do your chores,'* his dad had told him before driving off in their old Chevy truck.

Clint had just turned seventeen, with dark brown hair and blue eyes. He was a handsome young man, with an engaging smile. He was certainly an *All American Boy* and he was considered to be ruggedly handsome. The girls at school went crazy over him; but he certainly didn't go crazy over them. The one time he really went crazy was in gym class—and in the locker room—with all those half-dressed boys. Clint was always getting good remarks from his parents too, even though they'd never seen him out with a girl or otherwise dating. What his parents didn't know wouldn't hurt them though, as Clint certainly knew what he wanted. He had known since before high school....

Clint loved to sneak into his parents' room when they were away from the house and look at himself naked in front of the full-length mirror, drawing his arms into muscles and thrashing his waist around looking at his hard rod. He did have a nice-sized rod—one day last spring he had measured it and it came out to be exactly seven and one-half inches. He also had a nice patch of hair around it too. "God, I'm such a stud," he would say every time he felt up his meat and shuddered with pleasure.

That day, he'd gotten up early and let the horses out into the pasture, fed the chickens, and decided not to bother watering the vegetable garden as the sky was threatening rain. He felt good inside. He was thinking about his next-door neighbour Jason, whom he had known since both were just boys.

He went into his room, pulled off his dusty brown boots, and his white socks. He eased out of his black t-shirt and tossed it carelessly onto the bed. His right hand went to his left nipple; it was standing hard. It felt good to play with it. *Oh this feels so cool*, he thought. He played with it for a moment, then slid out of his faded *501's*. "Shit," he said, "I'm not wearing anything but cut-offs for the rest of the summer." He was down to his jockey shorts now. Laying his jeans on his bed, he slid his hand under the waistband of his underwear.

He went into his parents' room and looked at himself in the mirror. Sometimes Clint wore underwear, sometimes not; he didn't like to wear it, but he did like the way it looked and he knew that it was usually the last thing that most guys had on, that after they took that off he could see everything they had. He also found that when he was younger it made him hot to think of the other boys running around in underwear and then stripping out of it to nothing.

Clint stood about five seven. He wasn't super tall but he thought that he might have a few more years to get a couple more inches on his frame—his grandpa had told him that he had been short and not gained his full height until his early twenties. He had a very youthful looking face of course and still didn't have to worry about shaving to often.

Clint stood looking at himself in the mirror. He did have some hair on his legs, some thick dark hair which he loved to look at and feel. He ran his hands over it now. "Oh, you stud," he said out loud. "I'd love to fuck your brains out and suck your cock while I was doing it." Again he ran his hands under the band of his underwear. His cock was now very stiff, and he could look in the mirror and see the head of it and the piss slit through the thin cloth of the old underwear. He had worn this pair quite a few times, and the cotton was very nearly transparent. As his rod stiffened, it really stuck out in front and caused the leg bands of it to also protrude in front. This brought some of his crotch hair into plain view. He ran his hands now over his hairless chest, down and encircled his also hairless navel. "You sexy little stud," he said. "I want your body!"

Someone pounded on the door.

He figured it was most likely Jason, so he went to answer just as he was. He walked through the kitchen and opened the door. It *was* Jason.

Jason came in barefoot and wearing a pair of blue cut-off shorts, nothing else. He had brownish hair and brown eyes, and the way his skin shone in the sun, he looked like he was part Indian. He had a little chest hair and a nice patch around his cock area too. He even had a little around his ass hole He was eighteen, and taking a lot of the same classes as Clint, so they saw each other a lot during the day. Jason's hair was long in back—he liked it that way, long in back, parted down the centre. Jason looked down at Clint's condition. "All steamed up, eh?" he asked.

"Yeah...couldn't help it," Clint grinned, his dick pointing right at Jason, and now there was a little juice coming out of Clint's slit. He could see it making the fabric just a little more transparent.

"Oh, that boner," Jason said. "How cute. I am too." He dropped his shorts to the floor. He was now wearing nothing. He was rock-hard, too. It was about seven inches long, and it stood out so that Clint didn't have any trouble seeing his balls at all.

"Damn," said Clint, pulling down his underwear now. "Jason, you are so cute."

"You are too," Jason echoed, dropping to the floor and clamping his hand around Clint's dick.

Clint pulled him to his feet. "Come to my room."

"You know," said Jason as he left his clothes behind and followed, "it was so wild, all those years ago. Like when we went to the restroom and all, you'd pull it out to pee and so would I, but I never would look at you because I was afraid you wouldn't like me if you saw me lookin' at how much meat this friend of mine had."

"Yeah...I know, I felt pretty much the same way," replied Clint. "C'mon, let's go sit down."

They plopped down into two of the kitchen chairs.

Jason put his hands all over Clint. "God, I could fuck you a hundred times without stopping for a breath," he said, pecking him on the cheek.

"Damn it all," said Clint, "all those years we were kids and all...and we were too afraid to do anything."

"May I remind you that we're still kids and we're still together?" said Jason with a laugh.

"Yeah, yeah. I know. I just got carried away."

"I could carry *you* away," Jason said as he stood up. "Just like this." He picked Clint up in his arms.

"No, what are you doing? Put me down!"

"Stop squirming! Or you'll make me *drop* you!"

Jason carried Clint into his bedroom and put him on the bed. Clint's dick was still hard. "I'll be right back," Jason said and ran into the kitchen to get Clint's underwear. As he carried them back into Clint's room, he was breathing them. He took one long breath as he arrived back in Clint's room with them. "Ah," Jason said. "Nothing like worn underwear, he said, trying on Clint's briefs. They fit him too.

"Hot damn," Clint uttered. "You little faggot!"

"Yeah, and there's another!" said Jason, referring to Clint all stretched out on the bed. Jason pulled off the briefs now, rolled them up, and slapped Clint's tight ass with them a couple of times as if they were a towel. Then Jason dropped the underwear to the floor and climbed onto the bed with Clint. They rolled around to face one another and a shudder of pleasure coursed through Clint's hard body.

They kissed each other on the lips.

"Clint, I have to tell you something," said Jason.

"What?"

"You know I'm guilty of looking at guys, shit man, who isn't? But I mean...*you* are the only dude I care for. You are the only dude I've ever thought about. Hell, I've jacked off all day thinking about you!"

"I feel that way about you," Clint said. "Nobody else cares for me like you do."

"Shit," said Jason, "they don't know what they're missing."

Clint trailed his fingers down his buddy's chest. "Jason, do you ever...like to look at your hot body in the mirror?"

"All the time. I had a mirror put in my bathroom so I could see myself wag it around. When my parents are away like yours are now, you can come into our living room just about any day and see cum shots just hangin' off the ceiling."

"Damn!"

"Yeah," said Jason, "I like to take that thing when I shoot it off sometimes and just put it in a cup...drink it. I love cum..."

"Yeah I do too," said Clint. "I could give you my hot fuckin' load right now."

"I could take it from ya, too," he said as he started sucking Clint's dick.

Clint moaned in pleasure as Jason sucked on his hard cock. He felt around his own balls as he sucked. With all his touching, licking and sucking, within minutes Clint was shooting stream after stream of hot semen into Jason's mouth, and Jason savoured every drop.

"That's good shit," Jason said.

"Really?"

"Yeah. So hot 'n' steamy. Mmm...want me to give you mine?"

"Yeah... " said Clint now, feeling so horny that he was already developing another hard-on. *I barely lost the last one.*

Jason was unquestionably hot now, his boner had never gone down and after tasting Clint's hot wad, it had started dripping with pre-cum.

Clint's mouth was planted around Jason's dick as he began to suck. He pulled off one time and licked his balls, got them soaking with his spit. The two teens were in ecstasy as Clint now licked Jason's mushroomy cock-head, and went right back down on the rest of it.

"Damn," said Jason, "I love that. You make me feel so good. Aw, shit little boy, I'm cumming. I'm cumming!" He pumped out more juice than Clint could take.

Clint smiled. "I love it when you call me a little stud..."

Jason laughed.

Clint got his underwear and dried off Jason's balls, then kissed them.

"Damn," said Jason as Clint began to rub his sensuous legs. Clint pulled his underwear over his head and stuck his nose out the fly. Jason laughed. "You're crazy!" his friend told him.

Clint snorted at him with the underwear on his head, then took it off. "That was neat," he said.

Jason was still laughing. "You are just fuckin' crazy."

"Yep."

"Clint, have you ever laid in bed at night with a hard-on, and seen just how much juice came out? I love doing that and just smearing it all over."

"God, I swear I love you," Clint said, snuggling next to Jason. This was time that he treasured and dreamed about. Feeling the warmth of another male body against his.

"Oh, fuck, Clint, I love laying here next to you."

"Shit, I love laying next to you. But I *love* you too. Ever since I've known you, you've been like a brother to me."

"Me too," said Jason. "I never had a brother either. God, that's wild."

"Yep. But we're together now...and someday we'll have a farm of our own to work on. Just be the two of us."

"Yep, just the two of us."

Clint opened his eyes, still thinking of that time with Jason. He threw back the blankets, too hot and bothered to sleep now. His cock was hard, so hard that it almost hurt. With a sigh, he took hold of it and gave it a couple of slow strokes. He trailed his left hand across his stomach, to his nipple and he gave it a sharp tweak. "Mm," he moaned as he stroked himself more quickly.

"Oh yeah," he groaned, the bed springs creaking as he moved, "oh God yeah." He stroked harder.

The intensity of his pleasure welled up inside is loins until the orgasm hit, throwing him into a trembling heap as hot cum splashed across his chest almost to neck.

Clint gasped and lay back in bed.

Chapter Seven

"You've done good work." Clint tossed the cigarette butt away. He ground it out under the heel of his boot. "Done yourself a real good job."

Jesse just shrugged and leaned on the pitchfork. "I was just trying to earn my keep."

"You did that." Clint pulled some bills from his jacket pocket. "You earned every penny of this."

Jesse stared at the cash. "What's all this?"

"Fair wages for the work you've done over the last week."

"I thought I was working for my bunk and food?"

"You was...but you've proven yourself a better worker than I had expected. You've kept up with every task I set you. You earned this pay. Take it." His voice hardened. "I don't intend to offer it twice."

"Thanks, Clint." He stuffed the bills into the front pocket of his jeans.

"I should be thanking you for all your help in the last few days." He rubbed his chin. "You gonna be moving on? Still heading up to Calgary?"

Jesse frowned. "Well, I hadn't actually planned on it," he admitted. "Well, not right away that is. I got no real place to be after all. Not like I got any appointments in Calgary to keep. I kinda like working for you." He paused a moment. "Actually, I was kinda wondering if you needed me to stick around for a bit?"

Clint's expression hardly changed. "Guess I could use the help for a bit."

"Then I guess I won't be packing my stuff just yet."

"You ain't got much."

Jesse nodded. "I travel light."

"I'll be heading into town in the next day or so. You get your chores done before I leave, I'll take you along."

Jesse nodded. "I'll see what I can do."

* * *

Clint stood in the farmhouse window. He watched Jesse walk down the drive towards the road. For a moment, he wondered if Jesse was leaving, but then he gave his head a shake. *Not enough cash to live for long and he's not taking any of his stuff. He'll be back.*

Clint took a long drag off his cigarette.

Watching Jesse had gotten him hard. "Fuck, why's he do this to me?"

Clint rubbed at his hard cock.

He ground the cigarette out and plopped himself into a chair. He unzipped his fly and pulled out his cock. He started stroking it. Reminded him of a time with Jason...

"You ever whacked off with butter?"

Clint shook his head. "That's the dumbest thing I've ever heard."

"No it's not." Jason shook his head. He pulled his t-shirt off and then unzipped his jeans. "Sometimes you need a little lube."

Clint laughed. "You're crazy."

"I'm also horny." Jason stepped around the kitchen table. His erection was pointing towards the ceiling. "How about you?"

"Shit, I'm always horny around you." Clint unzipped his jeans, pushed them down, and stepped out of them. His folks were away from the farm for the day. *They're always away.*

Jason began to massage Clint's cock and Clint moaned.

The two stood there, stroking each other.

"I've tasted it before too," Jason announced.

"Butter?"

"No, dumb-ass. My cum."

"Oh me too." Clint was stroking himself, feeling a growing warmth in his loins. "Can I taste some of yours?"

"Sure...wait 'til I tell you I'm cumming...then get real close and I'll give you some."

"Okay!" said Clint, as Jason started jacking off in earnest. His mushroomy dickhead was really getting big and red. Clint kept watching that slit. He was stroking himself as well.

Gasping, Jason moaned that he was about to cum.

Clint quickly moved in close. His buddy shot most of his load in his mouth, and got a lot more right splattered across his face. It was a big load of cream that tasted really great.

Smiling, Jason bent his head close and licked it his cum off his friend's face. "Well," he said, "how did you like it?"

"It was good!" said Clint, licking his own lips.

"So how about some of yours?" Jason took a firm grip on Clint's cock and began stroking. Clint moaned and felt his dick twitch. White cum spurted out, splashing across Jason's nose and right cheek.

The two teens looked at each other and laughed.

* * *

Jesse knocked on the farmhouse door. The boards were weathered and the paint was peeling. A line of washing flapped in the breeze. Jesse turned his head, catching a glimpse of the Rockies in the distance.

After a few moments, the door opened and a woman peered out. Her face was weathered and worn by the passing of years, but it was clear that she had once been a beauty. "Yes?" she asked hesitantly. "Oh," her face softened as she smiled, "you're that new young man Clint hired on at his farm." She opened the door all of the way and stepped out onto the porch. Her hands were dusted with flour and a spot of white marked her nose.

"Yep." Jesse removed his tan-coloured hat. "Name's Jesse Coleman, ma'am."

"Constance Waverly. If you want to speak with Terry, he's out in the north field. He won't be back here 'til suppertime."

"Uh, no. I'd rather speak with you, ma'am."

"Oh." She seemed surprised, but then nodded. "Go on then." She brushed her hands on her apron, but ended up with more flour on them than before.

"Like you said, I work for Clint. Anyways." He stared down at his dusty boots. "I passed by this way back in the summer. I was hungry and desperate back then...running from trouble." He paused, chewing at his lip.

Constance waited expectantly.

"I was hungry and travel-weary and I did some things I'm not proud of." He dug his right hand into the front pocket of his jeans and pulled out several crumpled bills. "I stole some eggs one night and then one of your chickens. I also borrowed some clothes from your clothesline."

Constance said nothing.

"Like I said, I was desperate and did things I got no right to proud about. But Clint took me in and he's working me hard but fair. I got my first pay yesterday and I wanted to come here and make things right." He offered her the money. "I hope this is enough to pay you back. If not, I've got more."

"Oh," Constance looked flustered. "I'm not certain what to say, Jesse. Thank you." She accepted the bills.

"Is that enough?"

"Oh yes, more than enough for that old hen."

Jesse picked some hay from his checked shirt. "I'd return the clothes, but they're more fit for the rag bin now."

"Jesse, thank you for being honest." Constance took his hand in a firm grip, then abruptly pulled him close for a hug. "You've done the right thing, young man. A good thing."

He smiled at her. "Thank you, ma'am, for being so understanding."

"You have nothing to ashamed about, Jesse. In today's world, a bit of honesty, even it not 'til later, is still a refreshing thing."

"I should go. I got chores to be about."

"Good-bye then." Constance waved to him. "Come back for some homemade pie sometime. Tell Clint he needs to get off that farm of his more often. He's too reclusive. I'm glad that he's finally got a friend to talk too."

Jesse nodded. "I'll tell him, ma'am."

* * *

Jesse trudged along the road. It was hard-packed dirt.

An old black Chevy pick-up pulled up alongside him.

Clint peered at him through the open window. "Where you been?"

"I had something to take care of."

"Well, now there're cattle to take care of. Get in."

Jesse hauled himself up into the truck's cab.

Clint threw the old pick-up into gear.

They didn't talk all the way back to the farm.

Chapter Eight

Jesse read the road sign as they drove past. "Welcome to Nanton," it read. "Population 1500." *Small town Alberta,* he thought. *Not for me.* He longed for the money and the anonymity of boom town Calgary...or at least he thought that he did.

Clint pulled up to the side of the road and turned off the engine. "Here we are."

Jesse looked at the dusty street.

"Yeah, it's not much of a town, but it's the closet thing we got." Clint paused as he climbed out of the truck, to eye a tough-looking, ruggedly handsome cowboy riding past. The Marlboro Man stand-in looked like he could handle any ornery bronco. His big, callused hands held the reins as he sat in the saddle. His jeans hugged his hard ass and cradled his bulging crotch.

Jesse couldn't help but stare at him. "He's a big man."

"Seth there?" Clint nodded. "Six foot five, two hundred and forty pounds, or so he claims. "Works as a horse handler over on Terry's farm. Tough as nails, you don't wanna mess with Seth McCallister." He had such a presence about him, almost like the stallions he had been hired to handle. Broad and muscular, with a strong jaw and steel-grey eyes, he struck a very imposing figure.

"I wish I was built like that."

"You and me both, boy."

Jesse laughed. "This is such a one-horse town."

"And you just saw the horse."

Jesse twisted his head as he looked around. "Not too much."

"We got all the basics."

"A liquor store, a *Tim Horton's,* a drugstore." Jesse reeled off the names. "Welcome to Main Street."

"Post office in there," Clint gestured, "in case you wanted to send any notes."

Jesse didn't reply.

"The Pale Horse Saloon is just down the street. Sometimes has a good band on a Saturday night. Not often though."

"I should go and buy myself some new clothes. I can't keep wearing the same jeans everyday."

"Nope, ya can't." Clint took his eyes, reluctantly, off Seth as he continued to ride down the street. "Try Stedman's over there; other side of David's hardware store. He's usually got the best prices. Tell him I sent ya."

"Okay. Thanks." Jesse headed along the sidewalk towards the shop.

"Meet me at the *Tim Horton's* when you're done!" Clint called out. Then he headed for the local liquor store. He had a hankering for a good Alberta whisky *Gonna need it tonight*, he thought to himself. *Damned government.*

* * *

Clint was sitting at the kitchen table with numerous forms and papers spread across the weathered oak tabletop. He had a glass of whisky beside him, even though he had promised himself not to drink too much until after the job was done.

Jesse walked in, fresh from the shower.

Clint felt his chest tighten for a brief moment. The other man was wearing nothing but a towel around his waist and his chestnut brown hair was still dripping onto his shoulders. Clint looked up, nodded, and went back to work.

"What are you working on?" Jesse asked in that masculine but soft voice of his that Clint found himself thinking about all the time.

"Tax forms. The government wants to collect its annual share of blood from a stone."

"Oh." Jesse walked over to stand at Clint's shoulder, reading over it. He read silently until he noticed that his hair was dripping down on his friend. "Sorry about that," he said, taking the towel from around his waist and drying his shaggy hair more thoroughly while continuing to read.

The proximity of the other man's nakedness made Clint twitch, almost uncomfortable. Knowing he was standing only inches away, Clint took pains not to look up at him. He shifted in his chair slightly, hoping that would ease the swelling pain in his groin.

Jesse bent lower over the table. He gave no overt signs that he could sense Clint's discomfort, but he abruptly moved away and sprawled in one of the chairs, the dark brown towel draped around his waist once again.

After a few minutes he spoke up. "Clint, you in trouble with this farm?"

"Nope." It was a subject he had given endless thought too. Lots of family run farms had gone bust in the past two decades and it was common knowledge how hard it was to make a living farming these days. *One drought and I'd be owned by the bank.* "I've been running this land for years. It learned how to manage at my grandpa's side." Jesse deserved a good honest answer, but all Clint could think of at the moment was the fact that he still hadn't put on any clothes. He was being careful not to turn and look him square in the eye, but his peripheral vision took in his whole body—a muscular tanned form, with furry muscular legs hanging off the side of the chair.

Jesse stared into the fire for a while, then his brown eyes would move here and there, always returning towards the table to make a point or listen closely to what Clint was saying.

Clint desperately tried to concentrate on his paperwork, but his eyes tended to stray as well.

Jesse smiled at something.

Clint was trying to keep his eyes from roaming across Jesse's body, but he was unable to help himself. The best he could manage was to try and not be too obvious about it.

"Tell me something, Clint."

"Yeah?"

"Does it bother you? My just wearing this towel?"

"Nope." Clint hoped the flush on his face wasn't too red. "I've been a farm boy all my life. I've seen plenty of asses. Why should yours matter?" He tried to feign nonchalance. *Why* does *it matter?* "The hired help used to skinny dip out in the pond. So did Grandpa and I when I was a boy."

"Okay then." Jesse stood up, catching up the towel and tossing it around his neck. "Guess I'll head off to bed then."

Clint tried to keep his eyes on the paper-strewn tabletop as Jesse sauntered across the kitchen floor and down the hallway. He failed miserably.

The door to Jesse's room clicked shut.

Clint let out a low whistle and took a sharp slug of whisky

Chapter Nine

Clint wasn't sure if he was imaging things or not over the next few weeks, but Jesse seemed to be tormenting him. Nothing to overt, no obvious come-on lines, but was he...toying with him?

He seemed to go around shirtless more than was necessary. Coming out for breakfast or that last mug of coffee at night in just his snug boxer briefs.

Clint had grown comfortable enough to let his gaze wander over him as the other man walked across the room, or sat in a chair. His physique was really quite remarkable and the long hours working at the farm routine had given him muscular arms and a powerful chest. His waist was thin, and his stomach had a washboard effect. He had long legs with especially strong thighs from many hours in the saddle. Add in that hairy chest and furry legs and all in all, it was a body Clint hungered and lusted over, and woke up in a sweat at midnight dreaming about.

Jesse never seemed to mind that his boss spent long moments looking at his

body. Most of the time he didn't seem to notice. And when he did, it was just in passing and he never called attention to it by word or glance.

It was driving Clint crazy.

* * *

Nearly a month after Jesse had shown up, Clint lay on his bed. He was rock-hard and stroking himself. "What is up with that boy?" he wondered aloud. "He's giving me signals like a cat in heat...but he doesn't carry any of them out. Not like Jason...."

Clint remembered that day back when they'd been twenty-one as if it were only a few days ago instead of nearly eighteen years.

He and Jason had been out all day doing routine maintenance chores on one of the fences. The sun was hot, but the sexual tension that burned through Clint felt even hotter. Jason was bent over, tending to a downed piece of fence.

"Hey, Clint, come and give me a hand with this one."

Clint came up behind Jason, his eyes drawn to the worn denim stretched tight over Jason's ass. He moved to help with the downed section and his crotch rubbed up against those hard buns. Clint felt the other man tremble, then they both went still.

Jason slowly looked over his shoulder and the passion seemed to form a cloud all around them. Jason licked his dry lips, and Clint couldn't tear his eyes away from that tongue. It was Jason who took control of the situation. "Clint, I think we should have ourselves a little talk."

"Sure."

With that, they finished fixing the fence, and then rode down to their favourite swimming pond to talk.

Clint turned and looked up into Jason's eyes. He was relieved to still see passion and not anger smouldering in their depths.

"Clint, are you sure we should be doing shit like this?"

"Yeah."

"Really sure?"

"Yep."

Jason shook his head. "Well I dunno if I want to keep doing this."

"Don't you love me?"

"Course I do. You're my best bud. My right hand."

Clint laughed. "I like being *both* of your hands."

Jason shook his head. "I just don't know if we should keep this up. What would your dad say if he ever caught us? He'd probably shoot me if he knew I was even having these thoughts about you."

"We're twenty-one, Jason. We're old enough to know what we want."

"Maybe...maybe I don't know what I want."

Clint's mouth twisted. "I don't want to hear about your farther again."

Jason kicked at a clod of dirt. "He's been hinting to me about Betty." He didn't look up or face his friend. "He and Mom have been discussing grandkids."

Clint snickered at that.

Jason's face reddened. "Aunt Maggie just became a grandma and has been on the phone bragging about the twins. Mom's getting worked up. Dad's been pointing out some of the girls when we run errands into town. He...he's been asking a lot of questions."

"Pointing out all the *fillies* to ya?" Clint felt a lump rise in his throat. But his determination held strong and moved him forward. He'd had a tumble or two in the hay with young "fillies", but he knew himself well enough to know that just the sight of sweat running down the muscled backs of the hard-working ranch hands generated a hell of a lot more passion in him than all those encounters combined. He took a step toward Jason. Reaching out, he palmed Jason between the legs, and traced the outline of the hard pole that he found there. "What questions?"

Jason sucked in a breath and felt all of his resolve leave him as he exhaled. He lowered his lips to Clint's and totally forgot what he had just been saying. All he could think about was how Clint's wet kiss was making his dick even harder, and that no other kiss had felt more right. Jason folded his arms around Clint and deepened the kiss, pressing their groins together.

Clint groaned deep in his throat as Jason's tongue probed his mouth.

"Jason, you feel so damned good."

"Clint, I—"

"I want you so bad it hurts."

By the side of the pond, Jason showed Clint just how hard that he wanted him as well. They lay on the grass, kissing and groping and rubbing. Jason's hard body was on top of Clint's. Humping. Denim rubbing denim. Jason hurriedly removed Clint's shirt and jeans, and gazed down at his friend's sleek, tight body. Though he still had a boyish frame, his manly pecks were rounded and topped with twin peaks. The sight of Clint's nipples sent pulses through Jason's dick. He licked the side of Clint's neck and made his way down to those hardened nipples. Biting them gently, kissing and sucking, making Clint groan loudly. When he reached the hard cock bobbing against Clint's stomach. Jason let out a groan of his own. The pre-cum leaking from that perfect mushroom head, made Jason's mouth water. He dipped down and licked a trail from Clint's smooth nuts to the pool of wetness at the tip. "You taste so good, Clint," Jason whispered in a husky voice. "And I want you to feel good."

Jason spread Clint's thighs and pushed them back as he positioned himself between them. A shudder of pure, unadulterated lust ran through him as the puckered pink rosebud opening below Clint's balls came into view. He nuzzled the smooth, round nuts savouring the musky scent. Only another man had it, that scent he couldn't get enough of. He breathed it in deeply.

"Mm," Clint groaned.

Jason licked Clint's ass hole, slowly rimming the opening with his wet tongue. Then he began moving his tongue in and out, shooting thrilling sparks through Clint, whose ass hole pulsated in rhythm with the shaking of the rest of his body.

Clint pulled on his own nipples, making soft moaning sounds that blended in with the natural sounds around them. Jason fucked him with his tongue. "Oh man, Jason," Clint moaned, his cock sticking almost straight up in the air. "I...can't...hold it. I'm gonna cum!"

Jason's own dick was so hard, it hurt, straining painfully still confined inside his own jeans. He grabbed Clint's meat with one hand, loosening his pants with the other. Once free, his rod pulsed rhythmically, dabbing his abs with thick juice. He took the head of Clint's cock into his mouth and slurped contentedly, before swallowing him down to the hilt. He felt the first hot spurts hit the back of his throat just as the wiry pubic hairs started to tickle his nose. He squeezed Clint's tightening nuts as he sucked down gob after gob of the young man's tasty cum. He raised his head and went to kiss Clint. Clint kissed him back hungrily, licking up the cum that had dribbled out of the corners of Jason's mouth.

"Jason, fuck me now!" It was a command.

"Well, Clint, you sure you're ready for that?" Jason responded. Clint's words had sent a thrill through his gut, drawing up his low-hanging hairy balls.

Clint nodded. "Oh yeah."

Jason removed his boots and jeans. His balls were loaded. His hard, fat dick felt like a club between his legs. He was barely able to keep from shooting his load, just thinking about Clint's tight, young ass. He knelt between Clint's legs, pursing his thighs back again. Clint's ass hole winked at him, and Jason had to catch his breath. He stuck two fingers in Clint's mouth and had him suck them. "Now relax for me, Clint. Relax, cause I'm going in." He slowly inserted the spit-slick fingers into Clint's hole. Slowly pumping in and out. "Can I have this, Clint? Are you ready for me?"

Clint just groaned, his cock already hard again. Jason plunged his fingers in all the way, tickling his young lover's prostate.

Clint screamed out, "Fuck me, Jason! Please fuck me!"

Jason removed his fingers and positioned his erection at Clint's tight opening. "I'm going in, Clint. Slow but deep." He got the head in and slowly pushed his hips forward.

Clint let out a loud gasp as his hole clamped down on Jason's dick.

Jason was gasping too, it was so tight and so hot. It took everything he had not to just pound in up to his nuts. "We're gonna take it slow and I'm gonna give it all to you. Oh...you feel so good around me. I'm loving this."

Clint reached down to spread his ass cheeks wider apart as Jason finally made it all the way in. Jason's hips pumped back and forth, and Clint rocked his ass back and forth to meet him. Jason groaned and pulled out slowly just to the head before plunging all the way in. He repeated this. In and out. Slow and deep. They were moving in a sexual rhythm, in time to their grunts and groans. It felt fucking amazing, the two of them moving together.

Jason could feel the pleasure start to overtake him. "Oh, Clint, baby, I'm gonna cum! Hold on!!" He rammed his meat in as deep as it could go, and felt his body vibrating from his fingertips to his toes. He pulled out and shot thick, creamy ropes of cum onto Clint's young body. Spasm after spasm, till he thought he might dry up forever. He scooped up a fingerful of the hot cream and offered it to Clint to taste, then lowered himself onto him, binding their bodies together with his cum.

Clint was gasping for breath. "Oh God, Jason, that was too much." He wiped sweat from his brow. "I never knew it could be like that. I love you, Jason."

Instead of saying the words back, Jason kissed Clint on the lips, then pulled away. "Yes it was right good at that. But, I think we better get dressed and head on back, before someone decides to come looking for us. It's getting late."

"Yep," Clint nodded. "I'll be walking bow-legged for a week."

Jason laughed.

Clint ran his fingers through Jason's dark hair. "So tell me about these questions you're dad's been asking."

Jason pulled away abruptly. "We'll talk about it later," he said.

Clint nodded.

Chapter Ten

The dark sky was threatening a major storm.

It was already spitting rain as Clint rode up to the barn and hitched up his horse. He gave Railjumper a quick pat on his muzzle and made sure there was feed and water in their respective buckets. Jesse's grey mare was still missing from her stall.

Chewing at his lip, Clint stared out across the fields. No sign of him on the horizon.

A long, rolling peal of thunder boomed out.

"The horse will bolt in this weather and that damned fool will be left out there." Clint shook his head as the rain dampened his shirt. "I'd go looking for him, but where would I even start?" he asked aloud. His farm just covered too much land. "Surely the boy's got sense enough to come in out of the rain. If not, Misty will bring him home." He headed for the house, his boots squelching through the mud.

* * *

The rain was pouring down so hard that Clint could barely see across the yard to the barn when he stood near the doorway. He had the stove lit to boil up some water for coffee and he had a good fire built in the hearth to drive off the dampness.

Clint stared through the window into the night. *Damn, I can't see nothing.* Rain splashed against the glass as the wind gusted. He took his mug of coffee back to his chair by the fire. "Where is he?" Storms could be violent out on the Prairie.

A sharp peal of thunder made the old farmhouse shake to its foundations.

A horse whinnied.

Can't be Railjumper...wouldn't hear him from the barn. Clint got out of the old chair and hurried to the doorway. He opened it and peered out into the twilight.

"Jesse, that you?"

"Yep." Jesse appeared through the curtain of rain and darkness. He was slowly walking towards the house, away from the barn. He stumbled onto the porch, stopping to take off his hat and shake some of the water off the brim. He looked bone-tired.

"You sure are one sorry looking sight." Clint just shook his head, silently relieved that his hired hand had finally shown up.

Jesse was thoroughly drenched from the rain, and his shirt plastered to his chest, the tan cotton outlining every muscle. His dark nipples were clearly evident through the soggy shirt. His jeans were pressed tight against his legs and dark mud was splattered up to his thighs. Water ran off the brim of his dun-coloured hat in a steady stream.

"Where you been? I was getting a mite worried."

"I was moving the cattle to the other pasture like you asked me too. Took me a tad longer than I'd planned on to get them moved though. There was a lost calf in the herd."

"Come inside and get warm."

Jesse looked exhausted as he swayed on his feet. "I had to go looking for the calf. I couldn't leave it out alone in this weather." Thunder boomed out and made him jump. "Jeez, that's working up to be one hell of a storm." A second jagged bolt of lightning tore across the sky, illuminating the whole side of the house.

"Get yourself inside." Clint waved him closer. "You're soaked."

"Yep, I guess I am."

"Get inside. Don't you have the sense to get in out of the rain?"

"Most of the time." Jesse pulled his boots out of the mud and splashed towards the house. "I found the calf and got her home though. Frightened little thing."

Clint closed the door against the wind and rain. In just those brief few moments, his own clothes had gotten damp. "Get them wet things off at once," he ordered. "You're shivering."

"I stabled the mare," Jesse told him as he leaned against the wall to pull off his muddy boots. "Misty has fresh oats and straw."

"Always take care of your animals," Clint agreed. "But now you gotta take care of *you*." He tossed another log into the fireplace and gave it a sharp poke.

Jesse draped his shirt over the back of a chair and it promptly started to drip onto the floorboards. He fumbled with his belt. "Damn fingers are numb."

"It's too damned cold to be outside, you idiot." Clint shook his head. "Let me help you with that." He reached for the belt buckle and unfastened it. He unzipped the zipper and tugged the drenched *Levi's* down to Jesse's knees.

Then he realized just how silent the room was. He hastily looked up, away from the front of Jesse's white briefs. *Away from that nice bulge...* Looking up at Jesse's rain-slicked chest was little better, though, and Clint felt himself stir.

Jesse was watching him, with a half-smile on his face as he stared down. "You're doing fine," he said.

Clint straightened and roughly cleared his throat. "Hurry up and get 'em off. I'll get you a blanket."

Clint returned to the kitchen. He froze in mid-step.

Jesse was standing near the fireplace. He was still wearing his white briefs, but the damp material left little to Clint's imagination. Bouts of shivering wracked the other man's frame.

"Here." He tossed the blanket to the almost-naked man. Jesse wrapped it loosely around his shoulders and torso, then sat by down in a comfortable old armchair next to the fire.

Clint took a mug from a shelf in the kitchen and poured a shot of *Jack Daniel's* into it. "Drink this down," he said. "It'll warm you up."

Jesse downed most of the rye in one gulp and then coughed.

"Easy there," Clint cautioned, "it might be a tad strong for you."

Jesse shook his head and blinked repeatedly. "Damn that was good." He mouth curled into a smile and his eyes went glassy.

Clint chuckled. "Want another one?"

"Sure." Jesse held out his mug.

Clint shook his head. "I think I'll have one too."

The fire crackled and popped.

Jesse tossed another log onto the pile.

Clint lit a cigarette, then tossed the match into the fire. He turned to look at Jesse. "I think it's high time that you tell me your story."

"My story?"

Clint's eyes narrowed. "I lied to the law to cover for you. You owe me."

Jesse took another swallow from his mug and stared glumly into the crackling fire. "My folks kicked me out," he said simply.

Clint took a drag on his cigarette. "And?"

"And?" Jesse repeated.

"Why'd you get kicked out? You've been working for me for how a good month now? When do I get to hear the reason why you're running?"

Jesse frowned. "It's not much of a story."

"I'll be the judge of that."

Jesse sighed. "My Dad found out that I was being a little too friendly with other guys. I was basically given a few minutes to pack my stuff and then I was thrown out of the house. There was no real point in sticking around town so I headed out the highway to see what I can find."

Clint pursed his lips. "Too friendly?" His eyes remained narrow, but his mind started racing.

"He caught me and Phil in the garage. We'd started out having a friendly wrestling match...and got a little carried away."

"Got caught with your pants down?" he asked.

"Yep." Jesse nodded sheepishly. "We were stupid to try that with my folks right there at home...but, like I said, we got carried away.

"I'm not sure I would have been staying there after that anyway. I was already getting read more than my fair share of religious tracts on a daily basis."

"Ah." Clint whistled softly. *Was it just wrestling gone too far, or is he into guys? Do I dare tell him I like men that way?*

"Dad was ready to throw me out of the house. My mom said I should head west to Lethbridge and stay at her sister's. I tried, but that didn't work out either. Aunt Linda had problems with her own kids. She was just as bad a Bible thumper as my folks are.

"So I headed north. Eventually I ended up out here. Figured I'd go up to Calgary and try finding myself a job there. Maybe head to Fort McMurray and the oil fields."

Clint nodded. "Headed off with just the clothes on your back?"

"I had a few things packed. Got my pack stolen in a truck stop about three hundred clicks from here."

"Hitchhiking?"

"Yeah. I had to travel the roads somehow. Got a lot of rides from a lot of nice people. The truck I was riding in stopped for food and fuel. I was standing in the parking lot, having a quiet smoke, and got jumped."

Clint stared at him.

"There were three of them, a lot bigger than me. Dragged me in amongst the trucks, out of sight. Almost beat the shit out of me, 'til I came back with both fists swinging. They took my pack and my wallet. Took my leather jacket too."

"That all they did to ya?" Clint asked as he sipped his own *JD*.

"Yeah." Jesse nodded. "Gave me another, last punch to keep me quiet, and then they took off. By the time I had recovered my breath and stumbled back into the open, they were long gone."

"Did you report it?"

"Nope. What was the point? I'm just a drifter and I didn't really lose anything important." He gave a brief, bitter laugh. "I didn't have anything important or valuable to lose. My wallet was empty by then anyway. No cash or credit cards. They'd left it laying in a puddle, so at least I still had my ID."

"At least you weren't hurt too bad," Clint pointed out. "That's the important thing." He recalled seeing the fading bruises on Jesse's cheek and his ribs after he'd arrived. The torn and dirty clothes, the fear and desperation in Jesse's eyes out in the barn...yep, all made sense now.

"I guess."

Chapter Eleven

The storm was still raging and the level of whisky had dropped low in the bottle. The fire had burned down to a quiet flame.

"Are you feeling warm now?"

"Oh yeah." Jesse nodded slowly. His eyes were half-closed and his handsome face had a dreamy look in the glow from the fireplace. "How about you?" he slurred.

"Oh, I'm good." Clint wondered if he had drunk more than he should have tonight. *Hell, yeah,* he thought. *Good night for it.*

"I'm feeling warm." The blanket dropped to the floor.

Now that's a fine sight for a stormy night. Clint openly eyed the other man. The bulge in the front of his briefs was very prominent. "Ya know," he said, "I think you're more than warm." He stepped closer and ran his fingers through the thick hair on Jesse's chest. "I think you're pretty hot!"

"You do?"

Clint leaned in close. "Fuck yeah." He bent his head closer, until their lips barely touched.

Jesse didn't struggle or pull away.

Clint froze. *Shit, what I am doing?*

Jesse smiled at him drunkenly. "I like the feel of your stubble against my face," he said. He suddenly grabbed him and pulled him closer.

Clint kissed him again, full on the lips. The smell of whisky on his breath was hot, so totally fucking hot! Jesse returned the kiss with passion, his fingers fumbling with the buttons on Clint's red shirt.

The fire crackled.

Clint's hand moved down to Jesse's white briefs and tugged them down, along his hips. He ran his hands across the smooth rounded skin of Jesse's ass. "Fucking hot."

Jesse moaned softly. "Oh yeah, I want this.... I've been wanting a piece of you for weeks now."

Clint slowly opened his zipper and pulled out a thick uncut piece of his own prime beef. He knew it was nothing too special, but he'd never heard any complaints.

Jesse wrapped his fingers around Clint's warm hard cock and gave it a few strokes.

Clint moaned.

Then Jesse pulled Clint's jeans and his underwear all the way down to the floor. As the waistband of his boxers moved past his cock, the old cowboy's cock bobbled back up like a buoy in the ocean.

Clint pushed Jesse to his knees. "Suck it, boy," he ordered gruffly.

Jesse took the cowboy's cock in his mouth and sucked on it.

They staggered into Clint's room, still kissing desperately. Jesse's tongue pressed deeper into Clint's mouth and they both moaned.

Clint went down on Jesse. He grunted and began licking the other man's erect member. His cock had the smell of horses, cows and the range, and he loved it.

Jesse pulled Clint to his feet, then pushed him back onto the bed. He climbed into position and buried his own hard dick deep into Clint's mouth even as he ran his tongue over Clint's cock, locking both men into a sixty-nine position.

"You want that up your hot ass?" Clint took his mouth away from Jesse's dick long enough to ask the question but didn't wait for a reply. He sunk his lips over the head again and swallowed the cock down to the back of his throat.

"Oh," Jesse gasped, barely able to talk, "may-maybe another time."

"Ya don't know what you're missing." Clint rolled Jesse over onto his stomach. He raised the other man's buttocks high in the air and while one hand massaged Jesse's dick, the other caressed his back.

Looking back along his body, Jesse saw Clint lower his mouth to the raised cheeks and felt wet lips, then a wetter tongue, probe at his ass. The tongue seemed to find no problem going right inside. It hurt him slightly but the pain went almost instantly, especially when it was replaced by the absolute joy of the hot tongue probing inches into his hole.

Clint wet him up good and worked his tongue around in all directions, opening Jesse wide. Then, he took the mouth away. "I'll be gentle." Clint whispered, as he reached over to the nightstand for a rubber and slipped it on. His thick dick pressed up against the moistened hole.

Jesse felt it press hard and before he could gasp, he was washed with a thunderous clap of discomfort and felt the head pop inside of him.

"See, that wasn't so bad." Clint back drew himself back, out to the tip of his dick and Jesse shuddered. Then he shoved it back in.

Jesse was breathing rapidly now, grunting with each inward thrust. Underneath it all, he heard himself moaning. "Yes, yes, yes." Jesse raised his backside higher, pushed back onto the pounding pole. He sat back onto Clint's thighs, as the other man was seated on his haunches behind him. He rested his back against Clint's smooth chest, his head hung over Clint's shoulder. His eyes closed and his head swam in the totality of it all.

The dick climbed and drew back, struck home before withdrawing to its very stub, over and over again. Jesse was certain it was growing in size, beyond what he had he held in his mouth. He could now sense its depth, length, width, every ridge, curve, skin fold and vein. He charted it fully with his senses and came to know it more intimately than he knew his own cock. Amid the strokes, he felt himself being turned. Next moment he was able to wrap his arms around Clint's shoulders and sunk his face into an armpit. He sucked in a breath and enjoyed the flavours in his nostrils as it flooded to his taste buds. Opening his lips, his tongue drove into the hot well, under the muscular arm. He tasted it directly now, washing the jet black hairs he knew were there, licking up and over the smooth chest, along the ridge of tight muscle, forming the upper and lower biceps. Back into the hollow under the arm, he snuggled in and felt the safest he ever had. His fingers moved over Clint's powerful body, feeling the strained muscles as they flexed and relaxed, while performing the most wonderful action in and around his body, Jesse could ever recall. His own thighs hugged Clint's hips. The armpit was taken from him and he opened his eyes to find he was now laying on his back. Clint was still lodged inside him, but he was uncoiling his athletic body up and over Jesse. Hands took his thighs and they were raised, hooked over Clint's shoulders and his knees pressed into his own chest. Clint dipped his head forward, covering Jesse's mouth with his own and probed inside with his tongue. Their teeth clinked, tongues enwrapped and lips mashed tightly together. His body watched the speed increase into his back passage. Clint hovered between his raised thighs and pumped, pumped and churned, thrust and drilled into Jesse, faster and faster and faster. He tried to raise his ass higher still, to allow deeper and easier access. There was no need. Clint was perfectly aligned and taking him completely, utterly and in a most overpowering manner. Then, he stopped dead.

"If I keep going I'll drop it," Clint whispered right into Jesse's mouth.

"Don't stop." Jesse reclaimed Clint's lips and kissed him desperately. His hips screwed around underneath, trying to get that cock inside to move once more and remove the itch he was feeling, now that it wasn't fucking into him. He drew his ass away and then plunged back over the dick again. He could only release and recapture an inch or so, but it was enough to give him the sense of being screwed once more.

"You want me to blast your guts?"

"I want to eat your cum, Clint." Jesse begged him.

"Well then..." With that, Clint resumed his screwing but more slowly. He gave Jesse his entire length once more. In slow motion, he pulled away so only the tip held the door open, then slowly slipped inside until his hairy crotch brushed and tickled Jesse's butt cheeks.

Jesse lay still. His hands worked over the flexing arms either side of him, feeling their power. They glided across and over the expanding chest, along the rippling packets of belly muscles and down lower, to toy with the fleeting and advancing tool between his aching thighs. One hand found his own dick now and went to work massaging it, forcing ooze out of the head, which gathered over the entire length, making it slippery and noisy, as he jerked himself.

Clint slowed his action to watch Jesse. Then, he pulled out, so only the head remained lodged inside Jesse's butt, bent awkwardly and swallowed the head of Jesse's cock. Jesse bent his dick back toward Clint, working on the base of the shaft, while Clint sucked wildly on the acorn and neck. When he felt Jesse swell a little inside his mouth and more pre-cum seeped onto his rapidly labouring tongue, he commenced to stab his own cock end in and out, quickly, pumping the flexing ring. Now both cocks were having their heads worked on swiftly.

Clint knew he could blow at any moment, as well as knowing Jesse would give into his own needs soon. He lifted his mouth off the dick and drew himself free of Jesse's ass, then quickly spun around on the bed, settling his knees in, beside Jesse's head. He threw the soiled condom onto the floor and lowered his throbbing dick toward Jesse's waiting lips, which opened without any hesitation. His tongue lapped at the flaring head. "Taste that, farm boy."

Jesse licked away at it and finally gobbled the head completely inside, sucking feverishly, extracting more ooze out of the open eye.

Clint watched this with interest and once he saw how lost Jesse was to the moment, he turned his attentions to the quivering cock rising up before his own eyes. Their mouths sucked urgently, as each sensed that the other could fulfill all wishes at any moment. Clint heard Jesse groan, muffled with his mouth filled, while the dick in his mouth jerked and was pushed deeper by thrusting hips. Clint let his own control relax, rocking his dick back and forth over the tongue and teeth, devouring him. His thighs spread and his hips sunk, driving him deeper into the mouth. Then he let it flow. Clint had hardly begun to burst when Jesse lost his control as well.

Maybe it was the final signal for him. Maybe things were simply very well timed, planned slightly but fated perfectly. The lads pumped their spunk into the mouths of the other. Both swallowed because the volume was threatening to be too much. Both went stiff, holding all muscles in a locked position. Both made crude slurping, grunting sounds, as they expelled and received the hot man-juice into their mouths. And when the shots died down to dribbling surges, both took the other's dick in their mouth in a firm hand grip and squeezed whatever life's fluid remained, out from the fleshy tube.

Laying there afterwards, Clint held him in his arms. "You're fucking amazing, man." he said, looking at the exhausted, hunky cowboy laying beside him on the bed. "I've wanted you since I first laid eyes on you in my barn."

"So is being ridden like a bucking bronco one of the duties of being a ranch hand?" Jesse mumbled sleepily.

"It might be," Clint told him as he felt the aftereffects of alcohol and the amazing sex taking hold.

"Mmm." Jesse was resting his head on Clint's chest.

It was only moments later that both men fell asleep in each other's arms.

Chapter Twelve

Clint rolled over. The morning sunlight was pouring through the open curtains and falling across the bed. He groaned and reached up to rub his eyes. "Damn, I drank too much last night." Memory of the night's events came rushing back to him and he shuddered. "Damn." He opened his eyes fully and looked around.

The bed was empty.

The mirror on the wall reflected the otherwise empty room.

"Shit."

He rolled over and reluctantly climbed out of bed. "Damn it, I went and ruined a perfectly good thing." He pulled his boxer shorts up his legs. "Shit!"

* * *

After spending a few minutes in the bathroom, soaking under an almost-scalding hot shower, Clint stumbled into the farmhouse kitchen. He stopped dead in his tracks as he caught sight of Jesse standing over the sink with his back towards him. "Hey."

"Morning." Jesse didn't turn around.

That's a tad formal, Clint thought grimly. "I wasn't sure if you'd still be here come morning."

"I'm here." Jesse poured Clint a mug of hot coffee and set it onto the table. "Breakfast?" He wasn't smiling today.

"I'll just have coffee right now." Clint watched Jesse moving around the kitchen. By now Jesse knew where things were kept even better than Clint did. He was fully dressed in jeans and a blue shirt, even had his hat on. *Man, he has a cute ass in them jeans.* He felt seriously under-dressed himself, with just his jeans on. "Uh, about last night...."

"Yeah, about last night." Jesse wasn't looking at him.

Clint wasn't quite sure what to say. "Don't remember too much," he began.

"Me neither," Jesse told him quickly. "Guess that *JD* was too much for me to handle." He chuckled nervously. "I don't even remember going off to bed."

"Makes two of us." Clint gave a credible attempt at a sheepish laugh. "Must be getting old."

"Yep."

Clint stared into his black coffee.

* * *

Clint was making notes in his ledger. He hated doing bookwork, but the taxman demanded it. Jesse had avoided him all day...he hadn't even come back to the house for lunch. Now it was pushing into evening. *He's avoiding me. I've gone and ruined everything.* Clint frowned and threw his pen onto the table. *Why should I care? He's just a hired hand.* But they had both wanted each other so desperately last night.

The house was so quiet and empty.

Clint poured himself a whisky and sat back down at the table. "Just a hired hand," he told himself. "Nothing more."

The sounds of someone tentatively plucking at guitar strings drifted from down the hallway.

Clint stood up and stormed across the kitchen. He stared down the hallway of the south wing.

The door at the far end of the hallway was open.

Not in there! He hurried down the hallway, his boot clicking on the floor planks. He reached the open doorway and stepped through it. "What the hell you doing in here?"

Jesse was sitting on the edge of a bed, strumming an old guitar. He looked up guiltily. "I was just checking out the strings."

"That was my grandpa's. No one has touched it since he passed away."

"I'm sorry, I didn't mean to upset you." Jesse carefully set the guitar back onto the floor, leaning it against the bed as he had found it. "I didn't know." He shook his head. "I had no way of knowing."

Clint shook his own head. "This was *his* room," he said. "I don't like to disturb it."

"I'm sorry." Jesse hurried towards the door.

Clint stepped out of his path and then gave the room a quick glance over. It all looked fine. A neatly made bed, small table with a leather-bound Bible on it, half-drawn green curtains covering the window—curtains his grandmother had sewn—clothes pegs lined on the wall. Everything was just as it had been the day his grandpa had died.

Clint closed the door with a firm click.

* * *

Clint stared at the mirror on the wall of his bedroom.

A jagged crack ran almost the entire width of the mirror, about a third of the way from the floor. It had been cracked for years, but he didn't want to replace it. *Leave it the way Dad left it.*

Clint stared glumly at his reflection. "This is just what happened with Jason," he muttered. He went to the bed—his parents' old bed—and sat down on the edge. "We was just getting to really know each other and then he left me."

Clint still recalled the anger in his father's voice when he had caught the two twenty-one year olds out in the barn.

"*No son of mine is gonna be queer!*" he had bellowed as he hauled off his belt. "*I'll beat it outta ya!*"

Mom had said nothing, just sat on the porch reading over her Bible even more fervently, lips moving in silent prayer, as if that penance could cure her son.

"It's all going so damned wrong. Again..." Unwillingly, he remembered that last time out in the barn....

The barn had been quiet as Clint led Jason inside.

Neither of them said anything. They knew what each other wanted, could see it in the other's lust-filled eyes.

Neither of them was wearing a shirt, just their boots and jeans. Clint's smooth, muscular chest was sweaty from the exertion of tossing hay bales off the wagon and into the back of the barn.

Jason boldly put his hand on the front of Clint's jeans. He stroked the growing bulge with an eager smile on his face. "Oh yeah, you're getting hard."

"No shit." Clint's dick was harder than a rock. He reached for the front of Jason's *Levi's* and unzipped them. "So are you."

Jason pulled Clint's fly open and wrapped his hand around Clint's hard cock.

They let go of each other long enough to kick off their boots and drop their jeans into the straw.

Now nude like this, and knowing that they were both hard, they had suddenly opened up a whole new avenue of plans for each other.

"Do you like coming out here to whack off?" Jason asked.

"Course I do. I play with it a lot and I always think about you."

"Yeah I think about you, too," said Jason. He put his hand on Clint's leg. "Does it bother you when I touch you?" he asked.

"Fuck no! I like you touching me. It feels good."

"It feels good to me, too," said Jason, now rubbing Clint's leg. Clint started rubbing Jason's leg back.

"You wanna see me shoot a load?" asked Jason.

"Hell yeah!"

Jason was stroking himself. "I knew you'd say that."

"Don't I always?" Clint asked as Jason started jacking off.

Clint pushed Jason into the hay. He straddled his friend and they were sucking each other off. Clint moved his hips more quickly, pumping his erection in and out of Jason's mouth. His tongue ran across the tip of Jason's own cock, driving the other man wild with sensation.

Jason moaned out that he was getting close and Clint knew that he was as well

With a startled gasp, Jason shot his load in Clint's mouth.

Clint grunted and came.

The two lay in the straw.

"Fuck me."

"Maybe later." Jason laughed. "You are good."

"What the hell are the two of you doing?"

"Oh shit!"

Jason and Clint scrambled to haul their jeans back up.

Clint's father stood there, in the open gateway of the stall, shaking with rage. "I asked what the hell you was doing!" he snarled.

"No-nothing, Sir." Jason stuttered.

"Git the hell off my land, boy. Don't you ever show yer face 'round here again." He swung his hand and slapped the side of his head. "Git!"

Jason ran down the driveway.

"And may the Lord have mercy on your sinning soul, boy!" Clint's dad bellowed after him, before whirling around to glare at his son.

Clint hastily finished zipping up his jeans.

"Git in the house."

"But—"

"Now!"

* * *

Jesse had gotten the woodstove lit and was just filling the kettle when Clint stepped through the doorway into the kitchen.

Clint cleared his throat. "I'm sorry I got mad at you earlier."

"It's okay." Jesse rested his hand on Clint's shoulder. "I know you didn't mean it. I'm sorry I went in there. I was just looking around the house."

"Grandpa was a special man to me. I—I guess I'm just afraid to let him go."

Jesse nodded. "It's okay, really."

Chapter Thirteen

Things weren't okay.

Jesse had been avoiding Clint as much as he could. Sure, there were plenty of chores on the farm that needed attention, but even so, Clint knew that Jesse was going out of his way to avoid him.

"That other night was a mistake," he muttered as he paced through the house. "He's just a hired hand. Nothing more."

Jesse was gone off on some errand or chore, having saddled Misty Morning and ridden off shortly after dawn.

Almost surprised by where his feet had carried him, Clint found himself staring at the closed door to Jesse's bedroom. The long hallway was quiet—the house was quiet—and a feeling of neglect hung over the wing. *Too many old ghosts here in this part of the house,* he thought.

Clint pushed open the door and looked around the small bedroom. Jesse had made few, if any changes to it since moving in. The dark blue, hand-sewn curtains on the window, the rough blankets on the narrow bed...the same simple comforts his grandmother had given to the hired hands.

Clint paced across the floor, hearing the boards creak underneath his boots. He paused to run his fingers along the sleeve of a worn blue shirt hanging on a clothes peg. The front pocket was half torn off. *Souvenir of him getting beat up?*

Something fell to the floor.

Frowning, Clint bent over and picked up the small notebook. It had fallen open, about halfway through, and the pages were covered with words scrawled out in blue ink.

"*We talk a lot,*" he read. "*I'm not sure where things are going, but I think he's a great guy. He never says anything profound or does anything superhuman, but he's just a great guy. He doesn't work me any harder than he does himself. Never asks me to do anything he won't himself. I don't think I've ever heard him say a bad word about anyone.*"

Clint shook his head. "I shouldn't be reading this." But he couldn't stop himself from turning the pages.

* * *

Walking away from his Chevy, Clint gave his jacket a tug to settle the denim properly on his shoulders. The wind blew, gusting around the barn and tugging at his white hat. He lit up a cigarette, shielding the match with his torso. The sudden cold breeze was more of Alberta's unpredictable weather.

The sound of coughing echoed from behind the barn.

Clint rounded the corner and saw that Jesse was bent over the fence. He was coughing, each bout coming with a wet hacking sound. "You okay?" Clint asked as he picked up his pace.

"I-I'll be fine," Jesse wheezed.

"You don't sound fine."

Jesse coughed again.

"You sound like shit."

"It's just a cold." Jesse straightened up.

Clint nodded his head once. "Sounds worse than a cold. Probably caught it in that storm last week. I told you to get out of the rain."

Jesse shrugged, and then finished buttoning up his own denim jacket.

Clint frowned. "Maybe you should be in bed resting a bit."

"I got chores to do."

"They can wait."

"No, I should—" Jesse doubled over, with wracking coughs that left him gasping for breath.

Clint was alarmed. "That settles it. You're going to see the Doc."

Jesse shook his head, trying to get his breath back. "No, I'll be fine. I just need a little rest."

"No arguments, boy," Clint told him as the wind gusted around them both. "You're going to the doc's." He put his arm around Jesse's shoulders. "Come on." He pulled Jesse towards the Chevy.

* * *

Clint pulled his old pick-up over to the curb in front of the Doc's place. *I don't t think I've ever made the drive into town so fast before*, he thought as he killed the engine. He stepped out of the truck and hurried around to the passenger side.

Jesse had only just opened his door.

Shit, he's paler than a sheet. Clint helped him climb out, and then helped the younger man hobble towards the office.

"I can walk." No sooner had he finished his protest, then Jesse doubled over in a violent coughing fit that brought the strong young man to his knees.

"If I can wrestle a steer to the ground, I can carry you, goddammit!"

The handful of passers-by on the sidewalk glanced at them, and then looked away.

Let them gawk, Clint thought irritably, *I don't have time for them right now.* He half-carried, half-dragged Jesse to the door.

Clint kicked open the door with the toe of his scuffed boot.

An elderly matron looked up from behind a desktop computer, blinking her eyes repeatedly. "Why Clint Baxter. It's been a coon's age since you last darkened the door. What on earth—"

Clint carried Jesse into the office. "Morning, Dorothy. The Doc in?"

"Of course." She was eying the pair of them through her wire-framed eyeglasses.

Clint had expected such scrutiny from her, but he didn't care. "My friend here is mighty sick."

Jesse coughed.

Clint sprang out of the chair and restlessly paced across the small room. His worn leather boots clicked on the linoleum.

Dorothy had given up her earlier attempts at small talk and was typing out a file. Her fingers flew across the keyboard.

The sound of Jesse's coughing sounded through the door. It was loud and scarcely muffled by the heavy wooden door.

Clint took a cigarette and his matches out of his jacket pocket

Dorothy looked up from behind her wire-rimmed glasses. "No smoking in here, Clinton Baxter," she snapped good-naturedly. "You should know better. And why haven't you quit that filthy habit yet?

Abashed, Clint stuffed the cigarette pack back into his pocket. Dorothy had known him and his family since he was a small boy, and like an aged aunt, she always put him in his place. "Damn woman," he muttered under his breath. "It's getting so a man can't smoke no place."

Dorothy lowered her head back towards her waiting paperwork, masking her smile from him, and went back to her typing.

The door to the inner office opened.

"How is he?" Clint demanded.

Old Doc McKeller finished jotting down notes into a small notebook in his hand. "He some long-lost family, Clint?" he asked. Bushy eyebrows shrouded his dark eyes.

"Screw that, Doc. Everyone in town knows everyone else's secrets." *One of the drawbacks of living a small town.* "He's just my hired hand. And a good friend," he added after a moment.

Mark's eyebrows lifted. "Be that as it might, Clint, I have to ask."

"I'm likely the closest he's got to family around these parts."

Mark's lips twitched into a half-smile. "That's good enough for me then. He's got a bad case of bronchitis."

Clint shuffled his feet nervously.

"He needs a few days of bed rest. No strenuous activity for a spell." The doctor was writing something on a piece of paper. "This prescription should help him."

Clint tried to read the name of the drug and gave up. "Why can't these damn-fool things have simple names?" he asked.

Doc McKeller chuckled and didn't bother to reply.

"Thanks anyway, Doc. We'll stop by the pharmacist."

"And keep your smoking away from him. The smoke won't do him any good."

Clint frowned and pushed his way through the office door. "Like I just said to Dorothy, it's getting so a man can't smoke no place."

Jesse was sitting on the edge of the bench, buttoning up his shirt. "Told you I'd be fine," he said in a weak voice.

"The Doc's got some pills for you to take."

"About that," Jesse began, "I don't got much cash on me."

"I'll pay for 'em. You can work it off." Clint watched with great reluctance as Jesse finished buttoning up his tan shirt. "When you're better that is." He handed Jesse his jacket. "Come on."

Chapter Fourteen

Hacking coughs tore through the quiet farmhouse.

Blinking, Clint rolled out of bed. He paced down the hall, not bothering to flick on any of the lights. He knew every inch of the old house, even which floorboards creaked, and the varying sounds the wood made. Moonlight filtered through a shuttered window, giving the hallway a pale glow.

He pushed open the door to the room that Jesse had claimed three months ago.

The younger man was tangled in his sweat-soaked sheets and blankets, sound asleep. He was tossing, shifting positions as if trying to get comfortable.

Clint stared down, but didn't wake him. *He looks like a little boy,* he thought feeling an unaccustomed tenderness. *So helpless.*

* * *

Jesse blinked in the morning sunlight as it poured through the window and fell across his face.

Clint was standing in the doorway, watching him. "Morning."

"Morn—" he broke off into a cough. "You been there long?"

"Not really." Clint stepped into the room. His shirt was undone, and the button on his jeans was not fastened. "I was worried about you."

"You were?"

Instead of answering, Clint just ran his hand through his brown hair.

"That's sweet."

"I want you to get better. That is, I need you well if you're gonna earn your keep around here. I don't want no slugabeds."

Jesse nodded, his lips twitching into a faint smile. "I'll get on it."

"No rush," Clint told him gruffly. "You take your pills and get some rest. I'll get you some water."

"How about a match?"

"No matches." Clint shook his head. "Doc Mark said you had to stop smoking. It's just gonna make you cough harder."

"No smoking?"

"No smoking." Clint grimaced. "I suppose that means I gotta give 'em up too," he said sourly. "Can't have the smoke hanging around you."

"I'm sorry."

"You just get well." Clint turned and closed the door behind him.

* * *

"Hope I didn't keep you awake last night."

"I'm a sound sleeper."

Jesse nodded and drank some of his coffee.

For once, Clint was up first and had the coffee brewed before Jesse had gotten out of bed. "You should just stick around inside and rest yourself up. Doc Mark said you're not to do anything strenuous."

The other man grimaced. "I don't want to just sit around all day. I've been in bed for damn close to three days already."

"You're still paler than your under shorts," Clint told him in a firm tone. "You better follow the Doc's orders or else."

"Or else what?" Jesse challenged.

"Or else I'll show you firsthand how to rope a steer."

Jesse smiled over the rim of his mug. "That might be fun."

Clint snorted.

Chapter Fifteen

"You're sounding a lot better." He gave the other man a closer inspection. Seeing as Jesse had walked into the kitchen dressed solely in a pair of black briefs, it was an easy job. "Looking better too. Getting back that healthy colour in your cheeks."

"I do feel better," Jesse poured himself a mug of coffee. He took a sip, and ran a hand through his chest hair. "Those pills are working like a charm. I've never gotten over a cold that fast before."

"You could've warned me you got coughs like that."

"I never thought about it."

Clint reached for a cigarette and then recalled that he had left them in his jacket pocket. *And my jacket is hanging out in the barn.* He gave Jesse another studying look and felt his dick twitch inside his jeans. "So, feeling up to some normal work?"

"Sure. Want me to muck out the stables?"

"If you want. Just take care of yourself," Clint told him. "Don't push yourself so hard, Jesse, you don't gotta prove nothing to me."

Jesse smiled. "Sometimes I think that I do."

Clint turned back to his toast.

"I should go and put some clothes on." Jesse had gotten up from the table and set his empty mug in the sink. "Can't do my chores in just these." He gave his waistband a flick.

"Why can't ya?" Clint asked him, half-seriously. "Not like there's anyone here to see ya."

"Just you."

"And I like what I see."

With a grin, Jesse struck a pose and flexed.

Clint chuckled at the sight. "I like it." He stood up and walked towards the other man. The bulge in his *Levi's* was growing more prominent. "I like it a lot."

Jesse took a step closer. "I like it too." He reached for Clint's face and pulled it close enough for him to kiss.

Clint pulled back enough to speak. "Are you sure you wanna start this?" he asked, licking his lips.

"Yep." Jesse rubbed the front of Clint's jeans. "Hell yeah." He pulled down the zipper in a slow, gentle movement.

Clint shook his head to try and gather his wits. It was hard to do with Jesse kissing him while undoing the buttons on his striped shirt. "You've been stopping me."

"I wasn't sure." Jesse shook his head. "That first time...I wasn't sure if I was coming on too strong for you or not."

"Maybe we should take it slow then." Both of them were in just their underwear now, and both men were visibly hard.

"I'm sure of myself now." Jesse stroked Clint's hard cock through the thin material of his boxers. "I'm as certain I want this as much as you do."

"Are ya?"

"Fuck yeah."

"Come with me." Clint led Jesse down the hallway to what had been his parents' old bedroom. It was his now. He had to look at his body in that full-length mirror—had to see the two of them together now.

"Yeah," said Jesse, "let's admire the shit out of each other!" he beamed.

Still wearing his boxers, Clint flexed his muscles in front of the mirror. "Grrr!" he said as Jesse felt up his muscular arms.

Jesse laughed. "I want to put on some long tube socks!" He hurried back to his room and pulled on a pair on with his black briefs. He paraded back in front of the mirror. He did look good; anybody that could have gotten their hands on that body would have easily done so right there.

Clint stood there watching. "Fuck, you're hot."

Just then, Jesse walked around Clint to stand behind him. He took hold of his dick, stiff from all the observation and flexing and rubbing, and eased it into the back of Clint's underwear at the ass crack, and let it just kiss his ass.

"Try ramming it into my hole through the cloth," Clint persuaded. He did; there was just enough stretch in the cloth to allow Jesse to put the head of his dick with the cloth into Clint's hole, but at the same time it opened Clint's fly and caused his own dick to protrude out the front—it simply took all the cloth Clint had to offer.

Jesse pulled out and rearranged Clint's underwear for him, rubbed a hand across Clint's sweaty chest and pinched his nipples.

"Oh, you are so wild," Clint said.

"Yeah, I know, you are too," Jesse replied.

"Go put on a white t-shirt," Clint said, "then come back and lemme see how you look, you stud."

Jesse followed through with Clint's wishes.

Clint stood in front of the mirror, staring at his own reflection. *What does that boy see in me?* he wondered.

A few minutes later, Jesse walked back into the room, dressed now in tube socks up to his knees, his black briefs, and a plain white t-shirt. The tan that he had gotten from working on the farm over the last three months really showed against the white fabric. He smiled at the mirror, showing all his teeth.

"Fuck, you're hot," Clint breathed. There was a growing wet spot on the front of his boxer shorts.

"I want to stay here on the farm," Jesse told him. "I don't wanna leave."

"I don't want you too."

Jesse stripped off his t-shirt and socks.

Clint looked at every inch of his body now in detail.

Jason took Clint's underwear and stretched the band way out in front and let it snap back a few times. "Wanna fuck me, dude?" Jesse asked, his dick so hard that his briefs stuck straight out in front. He slid his briefs off now and threw them across the bedroom.

"Yeah, oh hell yeah!" Clint said, eagerly, stroking his already hard dick. "But only if you're certain you want to do this?" He certainly wanted too. *But I won't force him...I can't force him.*

"Fuck me," Jesse ordered. He pulled Clint's boxers down. "Right here, right now."

Clint fucked him right there in front of that mirror. Jesse grabbed a chair and leaned over on it. Clint got close and stood fairly straight, being able to rest his hands on Jesse's back as he pumped in and out. Faster and faster Clint went, all the time thinking both how good this felt and how good it had felt when Jesse pumped his ass. It sure wasn't long until Clint shot off, pulling out and letting his load splash across Jesse's fuzzy back.

"Fuck that was nice," Jesse gasped as he collapsed onto the bed. He coughed, but it was no longer the wet hacking sounds Clint had learned to dread. "God...."

Clint toppled down beside him. "Oh yeah," he moaned. He just smiled weakly at the other man.

"My, you look like the cat that just ate the mouse," Jesse commented as he gave Clint one of his boyish grins. "What is it?"

"Oh, nothing." Clint dragged his fingers through Jesse's chest hair. "I was just having thoughts about things you could do to me later on."

"Oh, like molesting you for a change?"

"Yeah," said Clint, still grinning. "Something like that."

Chapter Sixteen

"It's another wonderful morning."

"It's too damned early to be morning," Jesse mumbled, pulling the quilt back over his head.

Clint was standing in the doorway. Now he came into the room and pulled the blankets back off the bed.

Jesse was stark naked and half-hard.

"You've got chores to be about," Clint told him.

"What about you?"

"I'm ready in-case something pops up," Clint replied.

"Looks like something already has," Jesse replied, gesturing to the bulge tenting out the front of Clint's white boxers.

"Well look at that."

"I am." Jesse climbed out of bed. "I'll race you for the cold shower." And he half-raced and half-pushed Clint down the hall to the bathroom, both of them laughing and feeling good.

"You go ahead first," Clint said as he closed the bathroom door behind them. "I want to shave." He turned to the sink and started getting out the lather, blade, and so on.

Jesse climbed into the shower and turned it on.

As the steam started to fill his shaving mirror, Clint shook his head. "Hey, I thought you needed a *cold* shower." And then he laughed as he rubbed the mirror clean.

"Hey yourself," Jesse replied, "I thought you needed a cold shower more." He splashed water over the curtain at him. Before Jesse knew what had happened, a hand came through the curtain and turned the water setting to the coldest temperature. Jesse howled and grabbed at the faucet with one hand and at Clint's hand with the other.

They fought with the faucet until the bath curtain was half-open and water was splashed all over the floor. As they wrestled, Jesse managed to get Clint into a headlock and forced his face under the shower's stream. He was laughing.

"I give up. I give up," Clint said gasping. With that, he stepped into the bathtub and closed the curtain, straightening up under the gush of water. Jesse had released his hold on him and his arms were sort of sliding down from around his neck. He was still wearing his underwear, now soaked, but by his closeness Jesse could feel that his erection had not subsided at all.

Jesse looked down.

Clint looked down as well. He moved a step back and turned into the spray of water and then he stripped off his now-translucent shorts. "Guess I don't need these in here," he laughed as he tossed them over the curtain rail.

Jesse stood with his back to him. Clint looked closely at his muscles, at his tan line, at the smooth roundness of his ass. Clint wanted to touch him badly. Without turning around, Jesse spoke. "Wash my back?" he asked in a low voice. Clint hesitated a moment, and then reached for the soap. Working up a pretty thick lather, he stroked Jesse's shoulders and the backs of his arms, his strong shoulder blades and the small of his back. There Clint stopped.

Jesse leaned his head back. He let Clint's hand rest at his waist and slowly leaned his forehead in against the other man's neck. "Don't stop, Clint," he murmured as the water splashed down about their heads. "Keep going. It feels *so* good."

Clint worked his hand slowly down to Jesse's hips, rubbing in small circles.

He twisted his head to speak right into the other man's ear. "You've wanted to touch me for a long time. It's okay."

At those words, Clint felt something release inside of him. Clint knew what Jesse wanted and he knew that what Jesse wanted was really okay. Clint let one hand move around to Jesse's stomach, circling just above his pubic hair. His other hand circled onto his ass and felt the hard muscles packed into those orbs. His hand drew the line of the fold in Jesse's ass many times, working deeper and deeper with every pass, until his hand was reaching between his legs, tickling the bag that contained his testicles. Jesse groaned and moved his legs, spreading them apart.

Clint responded, pressing his stomach along the length of his side. Jesse put one arm around his waist as he submitted to the other man's touch and curiosity. Clint's own cock stretched across Jesse's stomach. As one hand fondled his balls from behind, the other traced the line on the cock stretching out before him. Both of them watched fingers run up and down the cock, pressing it this way and that. Then Jesse grasped it, first exerting pressure and then releasing it.

Clint moaned and closed his eyes.

Clint hadn't felt like this for a man in years. *Not since Jason.* Sure, he had fantasized about it often enough, but that was just daydreaming about guys he'd seen in magazines or passed by in town. But as both of Jesse's hands kept busy massaging and stroking, Clint leaned his lips to his cheek and kissed him lightly.

Jesse smiled and moved his head, making the next peck an off-centre mouth-to-mouth.

Clint leaned forward an inch more and they kissed for real, their tongues teasing each other.

As the water splashed about their bodies, their arms brought them into an embrace. Their erect cocks were pressed between their bellies. They kissed deeply and ground their stomachs together, breathing heavily. Hands found asses, tongues found tonsils, and cocks found stimulation until both men shuddered in orgasm almost simultaneously, clutching at each other's bodies there in the shower.

It took them several long moments for them to recover.

"Damn!"

Jesse nodded. "You can say that again."

Smiling broad smiles of contentment, they splashed each other's stomachs and hurried to complete their showers and shaves.

Chapter Seventeen

"Let's go for a ride." Clint made the suggestion after their leisurely breakfast.

"Sounds like a plan," Jesse agreed. He got up to clean up the dishes. His tight black jeans hugged his ass as he leaned over the sink and ran the water.

Clint put his *Stetson* on. "I'll go get the hoses saddled." He headed for the barn.

Jesse joined him there.

Clint had Railjumper and Misty Morn saddled and ready. The roan stallion was pawing at the ground. "He's feeling his oats today."

Jesse laughed. "Maybe Misty will be in a similar mood and he can sow some wild oats."

Chuckling softly, Clint shook his head.

They set out at a gentle canter.

"You ride a lot better now."

"I'm getting a lot of practice."

"Yep." They were riding the fences, checking to make sure none of them were broken or need of repairs.

"Always something to fix around here," Clint commented after the silence had stretched out for close to an hour.

"So what did you want to talk about?"

"Just stuff. It's good to talk about whatever's on your mind."

"Nothing on my mind." Jesse adjusted his hat to better shade his eyes. "You?"

"I just like to ride my land." Clint waved at the distant mountains. "I like being able to see what my family owned."

"You own *all* of this?" Jesse stared at him.

"Yep." Clint nodded and lit up a cigarette.

"You own all that land?" Jesse just shook his head as he tried to take it all in. "What have I gotten myself into?" he asked.

"I don't work it all." Clint took a long drag and shook his head. "Too much for one man. My grandpa, he herded cattle here. He made good money and relied on a lot of hired hands to do the work. My dad, though, was no farmer. He kept some cattle, but after my grandpa passed away, he sold a bunch of the land to other farmers, and the men who used to ranch for my grandpa, and he rented out most of the rest. I just honoured his agreements." *Like men were raised too*. He took another drag. "When I die, it gets divided up with the families who live on it. The rest, what I work, that goes to a nephew I got out east. He'll probably sell it off without ever seeing it."

"That's too bad."

"That's the way things is." Clint took another drag on his cigarette. "We'll head to the east a bit."

Jesse flicked his reins. "When'd you start riding this?"

"When I was a boy. My grandpa would take me with him to check the fences. I used to ride them alone when I was a teen. Ride 'em alone," he hesitated, "or with Jason."

Jesse frowned. "Who's Jason?" he asked.

"Just an old schoolmate." Clint frowned, then shook his head. "He left town a long time ago. Ain't heard a word from him since."

Jesse's eyes narrowed at the bitterness in Clint's voice. "He a good friend?"

"He was." Clint fell silent, staring ahead.

Jesse felt there was much, much more to know about this Jason, but now was not the time to ask. He just filed the name away in the back of his mind. *Jason?*

Clint gestured toward the west. "You ever climbed them?"

"The Rockies? Nope."

"Me neither." Clint spat. "Lived here all my goddamned life and never climbed the Rocky Mountains."

* * *

Clint yawned. The sun sure felt good beating down on him. "Let's head back to the house. Must be getting on near suppertime."

"Nah, it's barely mid-afternoon."

"Well I'm getting a mite hungry. We should head back."

"Okay, Clint." Jesse stood up and stretched out his arms. "Ya know, we're not too far away from the pond."

"'Nope, we're not."

"It's a pretty hot day." Jesse pulled his t-shirt away from his neck. "We should go for a quick dip."

Clint nodded. "Now that sounds like a great idea."

Under the blue of a clear sky, the two cowboys tethered the horses on the branches of a tree and then stripped off their t-shirts and jeans.

Clint felt good as he pulled down his boxer shorts. It was always exhilarating to feel the breeze on his naked skin.

Jesse finished stepping out of his briefs.

As always, just seeing him naked excited the older man. Watching him stretch his fuzzy legs and arms, bending this way and that, Clint's cock began to stiffen.

Jesse noticed this and smiled. "Looks like you need another cold shower, buddy."

"You could use one too," Clint shot back.

Jesse laughed and hurried towards the pond. He dove in, Clint following a few steps behind.

The water was cold, but the shock was refreshing. After a few minutes of energetic swimming, they both settled on a little grassy area nearby.

"That was fun." Jesse stretched out on his stomach and Clint lay on his side next to him.

"Glad you enjoyed it. I've always enjoyed playing in that pond." Clint stroked his hand along Jesse's back from his neck to his thighs several times before he responded by gyrating his hips slightly.

Then he turned over to expose his now-fully aroused cock. "I have other plans to enjoy myself," Jesse told him.

Clint stared at him.

"I hope you're interested."

"Oh, I sure am." Clint rested his head on Jesse's stomach and watched his hand at close range as it played with the other man's cock. Probing, stroking and teasing.

"Use your tongue on me, Clint," Jesse pleaded. The tone made it a request.

Clint continued playing with Jesse's cock, thinking about it for a few moments. Then Clint shifted a little closer and let his tongue play out and lick the very tip of Jesse's cock.

"Mm."

Clint couldn't tell just what he was smelling or what he was tasting, but he knew Jesse was liking it.

Jesse reached back and gripped Clint's penis in his hands. He stroked the other man's meat, rubbing the shaft.

Moaning, Clint let his tongue lick around the blood-engorged head as Jesse moaned and his hips began a gentle rocking motion. Trying it out, Clint rose above him and let the end of his cock find its way into his mouth. He rocked and moved it slowly in and out, while Clint balanced above, accommodating his movements as best he could.

Almost immediately Jesse pulled his cock away from his mouth. Clint could see that he was about to cum. Instinctively, Clint pulled his own head free from Jesse's hand and shifted position, so that he could take as much of Jesse into his mouth as he could.

Jesse gasped, his legs spasmed, and his hands grasped at Clint's back as he climaxed more powerfully than Clint had ever seen him do before.

"Oh my God!" Jesse moaned. "That was fucking incredible."

Clint smiled at him. "Wasn't it?"

* * *

They were at it again, like two hungry bulls that couldn't get enough of each other. It has been going on like that for weeks.

"What you want me to do?" asked Jesse.

"Fuck me. Fuck my brains out."

"Yeah...that's what I'll do." Jesse reached for the night table and pulled some hand lotion from it. He came back and rammed it up Clint's ass. Clint moaned as Jesse started to really pump it. "I'm gonna fuck your brains out," said Jesse, getting faster.

"Yeah, " Clint moaned, feeling Jesse's dick slide in and out of his tight ass hole and stroking his own meat. "That feels *so* good..."

Jesse pumped Clint with pent-up fury for a couple of minutes before he pumped all his hot sweet juices right up Clint's ass.

"Oh fuck!" Clint grunted loudly as he seemed to cum at just about the same time.

"Ah," Jesse said, "how was that, big stud?"

"I loved it!" Clint said, cupping his balls. Jesse's tool had massaged Clint's prostate as they fucked. It certainly had encouraged Clint's dick in the act of shooting out his juices, too. "God that was amazing." Clint's bed sheets were coated in his own semen.

As Jesse slowly pulled out of Clint's ass, Clint looked at his still-hard cock; it was coated with his own hot load. He instantly started to stroke his own cock, seeming like he didn't want to let it go back down. He rubbed it on Jesse's stomach and across his chest.

"Oh," Jesse started laughing.

"Ticklish?" Clint burst into laughter of his own.

"What are you laughing for? You're the one that caused it!" Jesse said playfully.

Chapter Eighteen

The blue station wagon pulled up the drive. A man in black jeans, black shirt, and black hat got out of the car and loudly slammed the door. He looked around at the farmhouse and the barn. "Hello?" he called out. "Clint?" Both horses were visible in the pasture, so he knew they could not be too far away.

The cows in the pasture mooed.

Jesse staggered out of the barn. He brushed hay out of his hair. "Morning," he said. "What can I do for you?"

"I'm Cecil Latimer, the local vet. Is Clint around?"

"He's in the barn." Jesse tried to tuck his t-shirt into his jeans.

With a knowing smirk on his face, Latimer walked past him.

Jesse watched him pass, admiring the look of the older man's butt in those tight black jeans. He nodded approvingly.

Clint stepped through the barn door. His red shirt was hanging open and he was just adjusting his *Stetson*. "Morning, Cecil."

"Morning, Clint. Already *hard* at work?" the vet asked.

"You know what farm life is like. Always something to do."

Latimer's lip twitched briefly. "I was just passing through and thought I'd stop in to see the animals."

"They're all fine. Misty has been acting like a filly half her age."

"Good to hear. I also wanted to let you know the horse auction is coming up this weekend."

"Already?"

"Yep. Judge got called out of town on business so he wants to have it done before he goes away. Going to be a lot of horseflesh there Saturday night. A number of prime studs."

Clint nodded. "Thanks for letting me know. I'd hate to have missed it."

"I reckoned that."

"I should take Jesse with me."

"Yeah, take him to town and show him the real beef."

Clint licked his lips.

Latimer laughed. "He not giving you any trouble?" he asked.

"Jesse? None at all. He's a hard worker, a good man."

"Always willing to lend a hand?"

"He'd bend over backwards for me."

The vet just shook his head. "Glad to hear that you've drafted a good *hand*. Folks in town wondered how you'd look after this place all alone. No wife after all."

"Not everyone is the marrying type."

Latimer nodded and brushed a hand through his moustache. "Why buy a cow when you can milk the bull?"

Clint shrugged.

"Have fun." Latimer walked away from the barn. He nodded politely to Jesse who still looked dishevelled, and then climbed into his wagon and drove off.

* * *

"Poke, poke, poke," Clint said. "Oh, I just love poking things. Poke, poke, poke, WHAM!" and Clint shoved his hard dick up Jesse's ass.

"Oh yeah!" Jesse moaned. "Pump me, motherfucker! Give me all you've got!"

Clint humped Jesse's ass like a bucking bronco. Jesse had his face buried in a pillow, Clint was on top of him literally fucking his brains out and in less than two minutes, he was cumming. Then he grasped Jesse's waist from behind, wrapped his legs around Jesse's, and hugged him tight. "God damn, that was great!"

"I like the way you poke, cowboy!" Jesse exclaimed.

"Better be careful, or next time you might just get branded!"

"Ow! That was terrible!"

"I thought it was kind of cute."

"You're spending too much time on the farm."

"I'm a cowboy, ain't I?"

Clint rolled over and then stood up. He stretched. "We should get cleaned up."

Jesse looked at him. "Still going into town then?"

"Yep. The auction's today."

* * *

Clint drove his old Chevy pick-up into town just like he drove his horse—hard and fast. He pulled up to the curb and the truck lurched to a stop with an awful shudder.

"I think the gears are going."

Clint shrugged. "The truck's older than you," he said half-jokingly.

The two men got out of the cab and stretched.

Jesse adjusted his hat. "So where too?" he asked.

"The auction house is over there."

The yard was crowded with cowboys. Lots of hot young ones there too. It was enough to just about make the both of them cum in their *Wranglers*.

"There's Terry." Clint pointed to him. "You've met his wife."

"Yep." Jesse nodded politely to Constance.

"There's the vet."

"Talking to the doc?" Jesse was eyeing the crowd carefully, trying to check out the hot looking guys without actually being seen looking. There were so many fine looking specimens though.

Clint paused to talk with the odd man, catching up on news.

One particularly tall and lanky cowboy was eyeing them. He had brown hair and brown eyes. He was standing near a shiny blue pick-up, resting his hands on his belt buckle. He nodded politely to Jesse.

Jesse turned back to Clint who was arguing with a fair starting price with two other men.

"You always underbid," said a man whose belly protruded considerably past his belt. "That's why you don't get the real winners."

"I don't have your deep pockets, Sam."

The man laughed.

"Few people in the town do, eh Jonny?"

The other man nodded. "Yes, sir. You got that right, Sam." He was tall and well built. His arms strained the sleeves of his green shirt.

"Been a pleasure talking to Clint, but I must move along. Other people I have to go and talk too."

Sam and Jonny pushed past Jesse without a word.

"That fat man runs the bank," Clint told Jesse. "Jonny's his right-hand."

"He'd need help to get past that belly," Jesse muttered.

Clint chuckled.

* * *

It was a fairly lively auction. Lots of bidding on the stock, and secret whispering and general socializing. People wanted to catch up on town gossip. The gossip was usually better than the auction, or so Clint had told Jesse on their drive into town. A lot of the current gossip seemed to be about Clint and his new ranch hand.

The auction wound down and most of the crowds had wandered off.

"You didn't win anything."

"Nope." Clint shrugged. "Usually don't."

"You could have bid more."

"Don't need more mouths to feed. Got just enough work at the farm right now for the animals I got."

"So why bid so hard on that one horse?"

"The white mare?" Clint smiled. "I wanted to make Jonny work for it." His smile widened. "Helped out Felix a bit too. Got him a few hundred more than the old mare of his is actually worth."

Jesse shook his head.

"I need a drink. Let's hit the bar."

Chapter Nineteen

"It was a good auction. Here's to all the hard deals won and the hard rides to come." The massive cowboy threw back the glass of whisky as if it was just a shot glass.

Jesse stared at him.

"Told ya Seth was pushing six foot five." Clint wasn't looking his way. "Try not to stare at him too much. Seth gets a bit...ornery when he's been drinking."

Jesse turned back to his own whisky He shook his head. "I wish I had arms like that."

"So does half the town."

The Pale Horse Saloon was fairly rowdy.

"Everyone's in town tonight. Everyone wants to party." Clint nodded across the room to someone he knew.

Jesse smiled. He turned his head and found himself almost touching noses with a twenty-something redhead.

The redhead smiled back. "Care to two-step?" she asked.

"No, thank you, ma'am."

Immediately, she pasted a pout on her face. "Turning me down?" she asked him, shaking her hips to make the folds in her skirt swirl over her boots. "So you can sit and drink with this old coot?" She placed her hand on his arm and gave it a quick squeeze. "Just one quick dance?"

"Last man to take her out on the dance floor is still missing," Clint muttered.

"You're just jealous that no one wants to dance with a bowlegged recluse like you." She looked back at Jesse and her voice softened. "Dance with me."

"Well."

"Go and dance with her," Clint told him. "We'll get no peace 'til someone does."

Jesse followed her onto the dance floor. "I don't even know your name," he told her as they fell into movement with the music from the band.

"Suzie." She held him close. "And you must be Jesse. We've heard a lot about you." Her hand drifted along his back, to his waist, and then moved further downwards to rest on his butt, squeezing gently.

Jesse jumped a bit as he felt her fingers tighten. "Talking about me?"

"Why, you are a hot topic." Suzie giggled and leaned in closer. "Mysterious drifter shows up at the farm of the local recluse and stays there? Course people are gonna talk. Everyone knows about Clint." Her words dripped with meaning. She eyed him closely, as if trying to catch him peaking down the front of her yellow blouse. "They wonder about you too."

"What about me?"

"Well..." she dragged the word out. The hem of her skirt lifted to show her bare legs.

Jesse just shook his head. "Folks should mind their own business."

"Oh, I know. But that wouldn't be human nature." Suzie giggled. "So we wonder and we talk and we gossip."

The band struck up another tune.

"You're a really good dancer," she told him.

"I need some air." Jesse shook his head. "Some quiet."

"The alley out back is nice and quiet."

Clint watched them leave the dance floor and head towards the back door. He gave his head a bemused shake and got up to follow.

* * *

"Feeling better?"

"Yeah." Jesse fanned his face with his hat. The night's breeze was cool after the stuffiness of the bar.

"Place is too crowded to enjoy," Clint muttered as he joined them. "The whole damn town is in there."

"I like the crowds," Suzie told him. "Not everyone enjoys a quiet backwater town like this." She turned back towards Jesse. "I like the lights of a big city."

"Like Calgary?"

"Just like Calgary. Go there every chance I get."

"What you queer-boys doing with my girl?" a voice demanded out of the darkness.

Jesse looked up.

Jonny and two of his friends were stomping down the alley towards them.

"They're just talking."

He turned his head slightly. "Shut up, Clint. Your fuck-buddy had better keep his filthy hands off Suzie."

"I am not your girl, Jonny." She shook her head, glaring at her erstwhile boyfriend. "Jesse's been a perfect gentlemen. *He* danced with me while *you* were off boozing with Mitch and Dave."

"Socializing."

"Whatever."

"God damn fags." Jonny turned his head towards his friends. "Swaying into town and prancing about. Got a fucking lot of nerve showing up."

Jesse nervously eyed the trio. Mitch was on the skinny side, but Dave was husky, his arms swelling the sleeves of his dark blue t-shirt.

Abruptly, Jonny took a swing at Jesse who ducked and then swung back his own fist in response.

Clint swore loudly, then took a step towards Jonny's friends as they moved to intervene.

"Stop it!" Suzie scolded the lot of them.

Jesse punched Jonny hard, and then he grunted as one of the banker's friends caught him in the ribs.

Clint stomped on Mitch's foot.

Dave grabbed Clint's arm and gave it a twist. "You shoulda stayed on your farm."

"Fuck you!" Clint wrenched his arm free.

Jesse shoved Jonny against the rough brick wall of the saloon.

Constable Daniels stepped around the corner. "What the hell's going on down there?" he called out. The flashlight in his hands threw a harsh light over the group.

The scuffle stopped instantly.

"Nothing, Constable." Jonny replied, puffing for a bit for breath.

"Just having a little chat." Jesse picked his hat off the ground.

"That so?" Daniels shook his head. "Better to chat indoors."

"Some chats you got to take outdoors."

"Men!" Suzie snorted. "Evening, Constable." She brushed past him.

"What's her problem?" Jonny demanded. "Suzie, get your ass back here."

She vanished around the corner.

"This is all his fault." Jonny hooked a thumb towards Jesse. "He brought her out back here to try and do something unnatural."

Jesse's face flushed. "What?"

"No man alive can make Suzie do anything she don't want to," Clint told them.

Masking a smile, Daniels nodded in silent agreement.

"She asked Jesse to dance, then they came out here to get a breath of air. This bunch came along and tried to pick a fight."

"Keep your mouth shut, Clint."

"Shut the fuck up, Jonny."

"Take it down a notch, boys." Daniels shook his head. "I don't want to have drag the lot of you down to the station tonight."

"Oh, no need to do that." Jonny shook his head, clearly cowed by the threat of a night behind bars. "Guess we just had a drop too much tonight. That's all."

"Law's still the law, Jonny. Big party or not, you're done drinking for the night." He turned to Jesse and Clint. "I think you two had better head home," he told them in a soft voice. "Just in case."

* * *

"I'm sorry I caused you trouble."

"What trouble?" Clint asked as he locked the farmhouse door. "Dancing with Suzie? That girl dances with everyone."

"Almost getting jumped by Jonny."

"He's got a temper on him. Swear he's dumb enough to try and stare down a bull."

"I'm sorry we had to leave."

Clint had his black shirt half-unbuttoned. "Don't worry yourself about it. We had our fun in town...now we can have some fun here."

Jesse looked up at Clint and suddenly he wanted this more than ever before. He knew that he wanted to be with Clint, and he let his instincts take over. Clint brought his lips to Jesse's neck, and started licking and sucking it, all the while unbuttoning Jesse's shirt, feeling the muscles in the wiry body he had admired and lusted after for so long.

Jesse could feel his dick aching for release as it pressed against his white briefs and the black denim of his jeans. Even through those layers, he could feel Clint's pillar of steely flesh rubbing against him with an animalistic passion.

Clint removed Jesse's shirt and brought his hands to the handsome man's nipples, pinching and tweaking them, all the while nuzzling the nape of his partner's neck. Jesse felt Clint's back, and ran his hands over his firm ass, kneading the strong cheeks.

Clint brought his lips to Jesse's and kissed him. Jesse was surprised at this, but accepted it whole-heartedly as he opened his mouth and shoved his wild tongue down Clint's throat, tasting the other man's tongue as it slithered against his.

The kiss lasted for what seemed like forever, but when they broke it, Jesse's pants and briefs were around his knees and Clint was jacking their dicks against one another in his big strong hands.

"C'mon boy, lay down," said Clint, leading Jesse to the bed. Jesse sat on the edge, and then lay back, spreading his legs. His uncut cock stood vertically, the foreskin peeled back revealing a wet, pink cock. His balls hung low and they were covered in short, curly, light brown pubic hair.

This was too much for Clint. He yanked the jeans and briefs from Jesse's legs, and stood back, looking at the blond, completely naked, except for a pair of white socks—which turned Clint on more, if that was possible. "Move up farther."

Jesse moved farther up the bed, Clint crawled on, and knelt between his legs. He stroked their cocks a couple of times, and spread Jesse's legs wide. He then ran his hands up them, feeling the smooth, soft, blond hair to Jesse's thighs, feeling the practically hairless part of Jesse's body while he bent forward and licked the very tip of Jesse's sensitive, slimey cock.

Jesse's back arched slightly, and his penis wobbled in the air, smacking against Clint's stubbly face, leaving a trail of pre-cum.

Clint grabbed the cock with one hand, held it steady, and wrapped his lips around the head.

"Ooooh! Clint, suck me! Give it to me! Blow my fucking cock!" He grasped Clint's head and started to thrust his hips into the cowboy's face, ramming his fat seven-incher down Clint's throat.

Clint let out a muffled cry as he almost gagged, but managed to get himself back under control, and suppressed his need to swallow. He fiddled with Jesse's balls, and slowly bought his other hand around to the little stud's ass, and narrowed in on the sweaty crack... Slowly, he inched his middle finger in, and found Jesse's rosebud. As he sucked harder, Jesse raised his ass off the bed, and inadvertently gave Clint full access to his asshole. Clint kept his finger pressed, and the ring gave. His finger crept in and was buried tightly all the way to the hilt.

Jesse felt Clint's finger enter him, and invade his bowels, and he started slamming his penis even harder into the man's willing, wet mouth. Jesse could feel his nuts slapping against his stubbly chin, and he moaned

in ecstasy as Clint fucked him with his finger. "Oh, Clint! Fucking yeah!"

Clint's ring finger just entered his butt, spreading him wider.

"Ohhhh!" Suddenly, Jesse spilled his load down Clint's throat, so much that Clint had to release the delicious bone from his mouth in order to catch his breath. Milky white cum flew out of Jesse's cock, splattering in Clint's mussed hair, and all over his hot, sweaty, gorgeous face. Clint grasped Jesse, and pumped him until the orgasm subsided, getting cum all over his hands too.

"Now that was great!" Jesse gasped, catching his breath, smiling at his

lover.

"It's not over yet," Clint told him with a devilish glint in his eyes. He pulled his fingers out of Jesse's ass, making the younger man sigh in content. Then Clint grasped Jesse's sock covered ankles, spread them, and bent them over Jesse's head, revealing the asshole he had played with earlier. Holding his legs back, Clint descended into the crack, and soon he was tongue-fucking Jesse, not an easy task since Jesse was writhing in lust, and pounding his once-again hardened pole. Clint pulled his face out of the sweet hole, and pulled Jesse's hand's away from the activity they were currently engaged in.

"What?" Asked Jesse, looking at Clint questioningly.

"Hold your legs back like I did."

Jesse obeyed him, and Clint spit into his palm, and greased up his swollen member. Then, with the utmost care, pressed it against Jesse's opening. It was tight. Clint grasped his tool and pressed persistently against Jesse until the head popped in and Jesse's entire body tensed up. "It's okay, just hold on Jesse...it's gonna be great," Clint assured him, pressing harder. An inch slid in, then another.

"Oh," Jesse moaned.

Soon, Clint was halfway in. Then all the way, his balls and pubes resting against the fuzzy ass cheeks. Clint leaned forward through Jesse's legs, and kissed the younger man. He could feel Jesse's penis thumping against Clint's washboard stomach, drooling pre-cum between them. "Okay, are you ready?"

Jesse nodded.

Clint held Jesse's legs back and started in and out motions of fucking very slowly. Jesse began beating his cock, and moaning as Clint picked up the pace so that his nuts slapped rhythmically against Jesse's butt. Soon Clint was panting and groaning, and pulling his cock almost all the way out only to shove it in so forcefully that Jesse was being slammed against the headboard.

"Oh yeah I'm cumminnnnnggggg..." Clint's cum surged out of his nuts and rose though his shaft into Jesse's bowel's and running down his thighs.

Jesse suddenly moaned with a second orgasm, and sprayed cum all over Clint's face and both of their chests. Clint flopped out of Jesse's hole within a few minutes, and he collapsed on Jesse, and they squirmed in the pool of Jesse's cum that was between them before Clint rolled off him. He turned his head and kissed Clint for the third time that night.

"The best," said Clint when their lips unlocked.

Jesse just nodded.

Chapter Twenty

The rain had finally stopped and Jesse left the house to check on the two horses out in the barn. "I hope Clint doesn't try to drive back here in this storm." It had been a nasty day, with visibility cut down to almost nothing in the driving rain. "He'd never find the road out of town."

Yet, the sun was breaking through the patchy clouds above, creating rays of golden streaks across the soaked green pastures.

Jesse splashed through the damp grass and muddy path to the barn. He pulled the barn door open and stepped inside.

A pair of jeans and a red shirt was hanging over one of the stall gates.

There was a figure lying in the straw.

"Who the hell is that?" Jesse asked aloud.

Neither of the horses answered him.

"Wake up," Jesse said. "Hey you, wake up!"

The man slowly opened his eyes. "Sorry." He sat up and tried covering his naked crotch with more straw. "I must have fallen asleep." He pointed to his damp jeans and shirt. "I got soaked and came in here out of the rain." He hurried over to his jeans and began pulling them on. "The rain was pouring down and I spotted the barn and ran for it. The door was half-open and the inside just looked wonderfully dry. I tried to see if I could find anyone and get permission to rest here, but I couldn't even make out the house."

Jesse nodded. "No problem," he said as he recognized the man as being the lanky brown-haired cowboy from the auction. "Not the first time someone's bedded down in the straw out here. Straw's warm."

"It wasn't the cold so much as being damp. I wrung my clothes out as best as I could...." They were still looked pretty damp though. "I was laying here listening to the rain pelting onto the tin roof above, drowning out all other sounds, and it put me to sleep."

"You were at the cattle auction the other night, weren't you?"

"Yep. I saw you there too."

Jesse licked his lips. "The name's Jesse."

"Jay."

Jesse extended a hand. Once his jeans were up around his waist, Jay took it firmly and shook it. He made no move to zip up his fly. "This isn't your farm, is it?"

"My friend's actually. I help out."

"Ah, Clint's hired hand. You sure look big and fit for a ranch hand."

Jesse wasn't sure if Jay was making fun of him or not. "What were you doing all the way the hell out here with that rain?"

"Thought I'd just drive out here and see my old friend Clint again. Left my truck down by the road and walked up. Used to do that as a kid and I missed it." He shook his head and gave Jesse a shy smile. "Silly thing to miss, ain't it?" He shrugged. "Sure took me by surprise when you showed you...thought maybe he'd sold the farm."

"Nope, the land's still his."

"Good to hear. Too many foreclosures these days. Lovely scenery for way the hell out here though. I notice you've got wheat, corn, and cattle." Jay made conversation as he pretended to wring his shirt out some more, but still left those jeans open, sitting on his hips. It was pretty damn distracting.

"Yeah, but not much cattle. Just enough for our own needs." Jesse moved from one foot to another, trying not to let his glances at Jay become too obvious. "Look, Clint's not here right now, but I'm sure he wouldn't mind you coming into the house to wait for him. I'll get you a dry shirt..." he looked at the furry patch showing, at Jay's parted fly, "and shorts, you can put on."

"Sounds good."

Jesse moved toward the barn doors.

Jay followed, carrying his shirt, while holding his jeans up, with one hand. "I never expected the rain to start so quickly, or come down so hard. I found the barn and the house looked dark and deserted so I thought I'd just camp out there until it passed."

"No harm done." At the front door, Jesse kicked off his boots and Jay followed suit.

Jay followed Jesse through the kitchen and down the hall and into a room toward the back.

He tossed his damp shirt over the back of a chair and dropped his jeans to the floor, standing there naked again. Jesse eyed him up and down, mouth slightly agape, then he realized what he was doing—and what he was announcing to Jay. He swung his head away and opened a chest at the foot of his bed, extracting a shirt and shorts from it.

Jay slowly walked over to the other man, hands on hips, delaying as long as he could, from dressing.

Jesse walked over and stood beside him, nervously, his heart slamming, glancing down to watch Jay deliberately scratch his crotch, lifting his hairy nuts and pressing his rather ample, low-hanging dick to the side, to better rub the crease near his hip and thigh.

"You been here long?"

He tore his gaze away from Jay's crotch. "Since the spring."

"I grew up not far from here."

"Yeah?"

"Yep. Left town as a teenager and only just now coming back. Passing through, most likely, but wanted to visit the old homestead one more time. Silly, ain't it?"

"Not really."

Jay gave Jesse a nudge.

Jesse nudged him back and Jay had a devil of a time keeping his balance.

"Sorry." Jesse gripped Jay's biceps and stopped him from falling over. He lightly slapped Jay on the back. "Not too steady on your feet there, Jay."

"You just caught me off guard!" He turned, grabbed Jesse by both shoulders and started a friendly wrestle with him. Jesse fought back, matching Jay.

Jay broke off. His fingers rasped into the hairy patch above his cock, making it lifted and fall, as well as swing back and forth a little.

"You got nits or something?" Jesse gave a cheeky grin and giggle.

"No, why?" He stopped his scratching. "Oh I just like the feeling of being free, ya know?"

"Yeah."

"So when's...Clint due back?" Jay ran a slow hand over his almost hairless chest, sunk it into an armpit, and then traveled it back over his chest and abdomen.

"No-not for a few hours."

"Then what are you waiting for? Here's your chance to let it all hang free, Jesse." His hand never stopped moving over his body, in a seductive way. He was making it very plain what he was thinking. His dick showed it as well, as it began to thicken, throb and rise up a touch.

Jesse backed away.

Jay frowned. "Sorry, am I making you uncomfortable?"

"No."

Jay took a step closer. "So you're just Clint's...hired hand?"

"Yeah."

"Nothing more?"

"What do you mean?"

"Oh come on," Jay said, "everyone in town knows that Clint prefers the company of stallions to fillies." He chuckled. "It's no secret."

He reached for Jesse's shirt and undid the top four buttons. "Yep, a nice hairy chest...that's Clint's type."

Jesse could feel his cock twitching and throbbing, growing harder in his jeans. "What the hell do you know about Clint's type?"

"I know what he likes." Jay stepped closer to Jesse and lowered his voice. "I know how he groans when you stroke his cock."

Jesse took a step backwards and fell onto the bed.

Jay immediately climbed on top of him. "I know how he grunts when he's got his cock pumping up your ass." He pulled Jesse's shirt completely open, his eyes glazed with lust. "Fuck, you've got a nice body, Jesse. Yes, nice indeed."

They didn't hear footsteps as Clint walked into the bedroom. "I made it back, Jess—" He froze in mid-step, his eyes going wide. "What the fuck's going on?"

Jay smiled at him. "Afternoon, Clint. It's nice to be back in town."

Clint stared at him.

"Been too long, I know."

Struck dumb, Clint just shook his head. "Jason," he finally managed.

Jesse blinked repeatedly. "*Jason*?"

"I was just getting to know your friend here. He's really a nice looking boy."

"What the hell are you doing here?"

"Is that any way to greet an old friend?" Jason rolled over and stood up. He slowly sauntered towards Clint, his hard cock swaying with each step.

Clint glared at him, eyes narrowing.

Jason laughed and picked up his jeans and shirt from the floor where they had fallen. "Think I'll go and get myself a drink of water. I know my way to the kitchen. Looks like you two might have a bit to talk over." He walked out of the room.

Jesse stumbled out of bed and staggered towards Clint. "Clint, I—"

"What?" Clint demanded.

"I'm sorry. It's not what it looks like."

Clint said nothing.

"I was worried about you in that storm."

"I can see how worried you was."

"He was taking shelter in the barn."

"So you brought him to the house for a cuddle?"

"It wasn't like that."

"Looks that way to me." He shook his head in disgust, for once not feeling any thrill from the sight of Jesse's hairy chest. "You can barely walk straight...he ride you like a bull?"

"Nothing happened."

"Cause I walked in!" He was getting angrier and angrier by the second. "Fuck!" he shouted. "I come home and find you with a naked guy on top of you."

"Nothing happened!" Jesse protested. "I swear it."

"Save it." Clint turned away, fury replacing the hurt look on his face.

* * *

Clint stepped into the kitchen.

Jason was seated at the table, once again dressed in his jeans and shirt, with a mug of whiskey in front of him. He looked up with a cocky smile on his face. "Hello, Clint."

"Hello, you son of a bitch." Clint's fist landed squarely on Jason's left cheek, sending him and the chair reeling backwards onto the floor with a tremendous crash.

In the sudden silence, Jason rubbed at his chin and looked up at Clint. "Still got that temper, I see." He still had that cocky grin on his face.

"That and more."

Jason stood up, wiping blood from his chin. "I came here to see you, not your hired hand."

"Didn't seem to stop ya."

"He was a nice way to pass some time, but he doesn't have your charms." Jason reached out his hand and ran it along Clint's shirt. "He's not you."

Clint pulled away. "You left town sixteen years ago. Without a word to me."

"Yeah, well your father and my father had some words. I got sent to stay with my aunt and uncle's out west before the weekend came. I wrote to you."

"I never saw any letters."

"Your dad probably tore 'em up."

Clint stared at him. *I threw 'em out. Unread.*

"I stop by to say hello and this is the welcome I get?"

After all these years and hurt of being abandoned? "It's more than you deserve." Clint's eyes rested on his rifle for a moment. "I loved you," he said, "and you hurt me worse than anything."

Jason shrugged. "I'm sorry, Clint. I made some poor choices in the past but I want to set things right now."

"It's too late for that."

"Clint...."

"Get the fuck out!"

Chapter Twenty-One

Jesse was hammering posts into the ground. Sweat was pouring off of him, darkening his shirt. He hammered away at each post as if he could pound away all of his frustrations in the process.

The sound of a truck echoed along the road, getting closer. He straightened up as the shiny Ford pulled to a stop and Jason got out.

"I see that Clint works you real hard. Do you need someone to watch over you and ride your ass?"

"What do you want?" Jesse demanded.

Jason smiled at him. "I just wanted to stop by and apologize for how we first met. I didn't realize you and Clint were so...tight."

Jesse looked back at the fence, silent.

"Want some water?"

"No."

Jason rested his hands on his belt buckle. "You're not from around here."

"No."

"Clint and I were an item years ago. We were best friends, drinking buddies, and more. A lot more. Surely Clint's told you all about the antics we used to get up too?" He gave Jesse a leer. "Once he and I figured out that we liked boys, we used to fuck each other every chance we got. I think we've had sex in every place on this farm." He chuckled.

"Good for you." Jesse picked up the hammer.

"We fucked in his room, at the pond, and in the barn more times than I can count."

"And you finally got caught."

"So he *has* talked about me."

"He's told me enough."

"There's more to life than this farm. Calgary's just up the road, and the oil fields can make you rich." He hooked a thumb towards his shiny new blue pick-up Ford truck. "No trick to that. Just be willing to work hard."

"I'm happy working here."

"Are you?" Jason nodded, though his expression was somewhat sad. "Then I suppose it's better to be working someplace and be happy than work somewhere else and only be wealthy." Jason turned on his heel and walked towards his truck.

* * *

Clint stood in the doorway of the barn. He turned his head as Jason's shiny blue Ford pulled up the driveway and rolled to a stop.

Jason got out and smiled at him. "You feeling more talkative today?" he asked as he closed the cab's door behind him.

"Nope."

"Good, same old Clint." Jason sauntered across the dirt, not bothering to avoid the puddles with his boots. He was wearing a loose green shirt and tight black jeans.

Clint frowned. Everything about Jason—his new leather boots, his designer jeans, wristwatch, and especially that fancy truck—said *I have money and I don't mind showing it off.*

"It's been a long time."

"Yep."

"Christ, you're not going to make this easy for me at all!" Jay snorted. "Fine, play the stood up prom queen then."

"Fuck you, Jason. You left me."

"I know...but I came back for you."

"And that's supposed to make me forget about the last twenty years?"

"Surely you don't want to stay here all your life?" Jason gestured to the farm. "There's more to the world than just this damned farm."

"This farm *is* my life." Clint shook his head. "This land has always been here for me. This place has always been here for me."

"I'm here for you now."

"That's not enough."

"It should be. Come on, Clint, what does this drifter have to offer you? I struck it big in Calgary. I can buy you nice things."

"I don't want a bunch of expensive toys."

"Stubborn as ever. You dig your heels in and a team of Mustangs can't drag you off." Jason laughed. "I'm just as stubborn."

* * *

The trip into town was a very quiet one.

Jesse headed straight for the liquor store.

Clint stopped long enough at the hardware store to make an order for some tractor parts. Then he stepped outside onto the sidewalk.

"Morning, Clint."

Clint turned his head ever so slightly. "Jason."

Jason smiled at him. "I didn't think you left the farm that much."

"I got work to do out there."

"Course you do. Where's your friend?" Jason looked around. "Let him off his leash?"

"Jesse's got his own errands."

"Course he does." Jason nodded and smiled. "Things to grope, I mean *get*." He chuckled. "See ya around." He walked off down the street.

Clint tore his eyes away from the sight of Jason's butt—his dark blue *Buffalo* jeans were skin-tight—and looked around for Jesse.

Jesse stepped out of the liquor store with a smile on his face.

Clint's eyes narrowed as a young man followed him out. They were both laughing at some shared joke.

Jesse spotted Clint walking towards him and his smile slipped.

Clint pushed past them without a word.

Chapter Twenty-Two

Jesse stood on the porch of the farmhouse and stared across the yard at the blue Ford. It was sitting outside of the barn yet again, gleaming in the afternoon sun. The two of them were in there. It was driving Jesse crazy, not knowing...were they just talking, in there, or was something more going on? Were Clint and his long-lost buddy going to get back together? Where would that leave him?

A million questions raced through his mind as he anxiously paced back and forth. He lit a cigarette, knowing he shouldn't be smoking, but unable to stop himself. Shit!

Jesse flung the half-smoked cigarette into the dirt and strode across the yard. He had to know!

The barn door was standing open.

Jason was standing near one of the stalls, his back to the door. "That drifter can't offer you anything. He's still just a kid."

"Jesse is a very hard worker." Clint was out of sight, apparently working inside one of the stalls. "He's made things easier."

"We had something good, Clint."

"Yeah, *had*. That was then, this is now. Things change."

"You remember that day out by the pond? We'd been fixing the fence and stopped there for a quick dip to cool off? You told me that you loved me."

"You didn't say it back."

"I know...I was scared too. I wasn't used to having those kinds of feelings for anyone. You know what my folks were like...just like yours. They wouldn't have accepted you and me. Dad would shown up here with his rifle."

"So you slipped out of town."

"I made something of myself." Jason sounded proud. "I went to the oil fields and I worked hard and I made something of myself."

"And now you're back?"

"I came back for you."

Clint snorted.

"I've got a house in Calgary, a real nice house. I've got money. You've seen my truck...a lot newer than anything you've ever driven."

"So why waste your time coming out here?"

"Because I'm lonely. What's the point in having a big house when you live alone? What's the point of having all that cash if you don't have anyone to spend it on?"

"What's the point of—"

"Damn it, Clint, I love you!" There was a moment of dead silence before Jason continued. "I think I've always loved you...I just couldn't say it before."

Unwilling to listen any longer, Jesse turned away and ran back towards the farmhouse.

* * *

A mug of whiskey in his hand, Jesse stood at the kitchen window and watched Jason walk out of the barn and climb into his Ford. As the truck pulled away, he spun tires on dirt.

Jesse swallowed the whiskey in one long gulp.

Feet shuffling, Jesse walked into his room. He pulled off his t-shirt and stuffed it into his denim knapsack. He pulled shirts and jeans from the pegs on the wall and stuffed them into his pack as well, his eyes blurring with tears. Taking another shirt from the peg, he let it drop to the floor and sank onto the bed, stifling a sob that tore up from his throat.

Clint walked into the bedroom and stopped dead. "What the hell are you doing?" he demanded after a moment.

Jesse was still sitting on the edge of the bed in his torn jeans. "Looks like you don't need me around here any more. I'm just packing up." He held his Stetson in his hands, staring glumly at it.

Clint leaned against the wall and lit up a cigarette.

The silence stretched out interminably. Seconds turned into minutes. Clint's cigarette smoke filled the air. Neither of them moved.

"I'm sorry," Jesse said quietly.

"Me too." Clint took a drag. "Jason is leaving town again." He paused a moment. "He's not coming back."

Jesse lifted his gaze to look at his friend. "Wh-what? He's not staying here?"

"Nope. What the two of us had was a long time ago. It's over and done with. What you and I have is more. Something better. I hope."

"So what does this mean for us?" Jesse asked softly.

"What do you want it to mean?"

"I want—I want to be with you." Jesse's voice cracked as he spoke. "I don't want to lose you."

"I want the same thing." Clint put his arm on Jesse's shoulder. "You and me, buddy."

Jesse grabbed him a fierce hug. "I, I—" Tears ran down his cheeks.

Clint frowned, and then he hugged back just as fiercely. "I want you and only you."

Also by Frank Sol

Novels Of The Sensual City
A Family Affair

Novels On The Prairies
Bareback Range
Return To Bareback Range
Fenced In